"DEAR AMY

This money is from your father. I have not seen him or heard from him since four months before you were born, but two weeks after you were born I received a bank check for one thousand dollars in the mail, and I have received one every month since then . . ."

That's how Amy Denovo ended up with a quarter of a million dollars' worth of skins in her closet. But even if she offered me the whole bag, I didn't like the idea of trying to find her father . . . because it was beginning to look as if he had murdered her mother.

THE FATHER HUNT

The Father Hunt
by Rex Stout

A Nero Wolfe Mystery

BANTAM BOOKS
TORONTO • NEW YORK • LONDON • SYDNEY • AUCKLAND

*This low-priced Bantam Book
has been completely reset in a type face
designed for easy reading, and was printed
from new plates. It contains the complete
text of the original hard-cover edition.*
NOT ONE WORD HAS BEEN OMITTED.

THE FATHER HUNT

*A Bantam Book / published by arrangement with
The Viking Press*

PRINTING HISTORY

Viking edition published May 1968

Mystery Guild edition published August 1968

Bantam edition / June 1969

2nd printing ...... July 1969	6th printing ...... July 1971
3rd printing ... October 1969	7th printing ... October 1972
4th printing ..... March 1970	8th printing ... October 1974
5th printing ..... March 1971	9th printing .. December 1980
	10th printing ... November 1984

ISBN 0-553-24728-X

Published simultaneously in the United States and Canada

Bantam Books are published by Bantam Books, Inc. Its trademark, consisting of the words "Bantam Books" and the por-
trayal of a rooster, is Registered in U.S. Patent and Trademark
Office and in other countries. Marca Registrada. Bantam
Books, Inc., 666 Fifth Avenue, New York, New York 10103.

PRINTED IN THE UNITED STATES OF AMERICA

H   19 18 17 16 15 14 13 12 11 10

1

It happens once or twice a week. Lily Rowan and I, returning from a show or party or hockey game, leave the elevator and approach the door of her penthouse on top of the apartment building on Sixty-third Street between Madison and Park, and there is the key question. Mine is, Do I stay back and let her do it? Hers is, Does she stay back and let me do it? We have never discussed it, and it is always handled the same way. When she gets out her key as we leave the elevator she gives me a smile which means, "Yes, you have one, but it's my door," and I smile back and follow her to it. It is understood that mine is for situations that seldom arise.

That Thursday afternoon in August we had been to Shea Stadium to watch the Mets clobber the Giants, which they had done, 8 to 3, and it was only twenty past five when she used her key. Inside, she called out to Mimi, the maid, that she was home, and went to the bathroom, and I went to the bar in a corner of the oversized living room, with its 19-by-34 Kashan rug, for gin and ice and tonic and glasses. By the time I got out to the terrace with the tray she was there, at a table under the awning, studying the scorecard I had kept.

"Yes, sir," she said as I put the tray down, "Harrelson got three hits and batted in two runs. If he was here I'd hug him. Good."

"Then I'm glad he's not here." I gave her her drink and sat. "If you hugged that kid good you'd crack a rib."

A voice came. "I'm going, Miss Rowan."

Our heads turned. The young woman in the doorway to the living room was a newcomer to the penthouse. I had seen her only twice, and she was easy to look at, with just enough round places, just round enough, properly spotted on her five-foot-four getup, and her warm dark skin just right for her quick brown eyes. Her dark-brown hair was bunched at the back. Her name was Amy Denovo and she had got a diploma from Smith in June. Lily had hired her ten days ago, at a hundred a week, to help her find and arrange material for a book a man was going to write about Lily's father, who had made a pile building sewers and other items and had left her enough boodle to keep a dozen penthouses.

She answered a couple of questions Lily asked, and left, and we talked baseball, concentrating on what the Mets had, if anything, besides Tommy Davis and Bud Harrelson and Tom Seaver, and what they might have if we lived long enough. We dawdled with the drinks, and at six o'clock I got up to go, leaving Lily plenty of time to change for a dinner she had been hooked for, where people were going to abolish ghettos by making speeches. I had a date, later, where I intended to abolish the welfare of some friends of mine by drawing another ace or maybe jack.

But down in the lobby I was intercepted. Albert, the doorman, was moving to open the door for me when a voice spoke my name and I turned, and Amy Denovo left a chair and was coming. She gave me a nice little smile and said, "Could you give me a few minutes to ask you something?"

I said, "Sure, shoot," and she glanced at Albert, and he took the hint and went outside. I said we might as well sit and we went to a bench at the wall, but the door opened again and a man and woman entered, crossed to the elevator, and stood.

Amy Denovo said, "It *is* rather public, isn't it? I said a few minutes, but I suppose . . . it might be more than just a few. If you could? And I . . . it's very personal. . . . I mean personal to me."

I hadn't noticed the dimples before. They are always more taking on a dark skin than on a light skin. "You're twenty-two," I said.

She nodded.

"Then maybe one minute will do it. Don't marry him

now, you're too young to know. Wait a year at least, and—"

"Oh, it isn't that! It's *very* personal."

"Don't think marriage isn't personal. It's too damn personal, that's the trouble. If you mean a few hours, not a few minutes, I'm sorry; I have an eight o'clock date, but there's a place around the corner that sells drinks and makes good egg-and-anchovy sandwiches. If you like anchovies."

"I do."

The door opened and two women entered and headed for the elevator. That was not the place to discuss *very* personal matters.

She was all right to walk with, no leading or lagging and no silly step-stretching. At that time of day in August there was plenty of room in the back at The Cooler, and we got the corner table where Lily and I had often had a snack. When the waitress had taken our order and left, I asked if she wanted to put off being personal until we had something inside.

She shook her head. "I might as well . . ." She let it hang ten seconds and then blurted, "I want you to find my father."

I raised a brow. "Have you lost him?"

"No. I haven't lost him . . . because I never had him." She said it fast, as if someone was trying to stop her. "I decided I had to tell somebody—that was a month ago— and then I got this job with Miss Rowan and I found out that she knows you, and I met you, and of course I know about you and Nero Wolfe. But I don't want Nero Wolfe to do it, I want you to."

There were no dimples, and the quick brown eyes were fastened on me.

"That won't work," I told her. "I'm on full time with Mr. Wolfe, twenty-four hours a day and seven days a week when they're needed, and I don't take jobs on my own. But I have a loose hour"—I looked at my watch— "and twenty minutes, and if you want a suggestion I might possibly have one. No charge."

"But I need more than a suggestion."

"You're not in a position to judge. You're too involved."

"I'm involved all right." The eyes stayed at me. "I

couldn't tell this to anybody but you. Not *anybody*. When
I met you last week, the first time, I felt it then, I knew it,
that you were the one man in the world that I could trust
to do it. I never had that feeling about a man before—or
woman either."

"That's just dandy," I said, "but save the soap. Did you
say you never had your father?"

Her eyes darted away as the waitress came with the
drinks and sandwiches. When we had been served and
were alone again she tried to smile. "That wasn't just
figurative." She kept her voice low and I needed my good
ears. "I meant that literally. I never had a father. I don't
know who he was. Is. I don't know what my name is, what
it should be. Nobody knows about it—*nobody*. Now you
know. I don't think Denovo was my mother's real name.
I don't think she was ever married. Do you know what
Denovo means? Two Latin words, *de novo?*"

"Something about new. A nova is a new star."

"It means 'anew.' 'Afresh.' She started anew, afresh,
she started over, and she took the name Denovo. I wish
I knew for sure."

"Have you asked her?"

"No. I wanted to, I was going to, and now I can't.
She's dead."

"When did she die?"

"In May. Just two weeks before I graduated. By a car.
A hit-and-run driver."

"Did they get him?"

"No. They haven't found him. They are still looking;
they say they are."

"What about relatives? A sister, a brother . . ."

"There aren't any."

"There must be. Everyone has relatives."

"No. None. Of course there might be some under her
real name."

"Have you got any? Cousins, uncles, aunts . . ."

"No."

It was getting messy. Or rather, it was getting too damn
pure and simple. I knew people who liked to think of
themselves as loners, but Amy Denovo really was one;
with her it wasn't just thinking. I suggested that we might
try the sandwiches, and she agreed and took one, and took

a bite. Naturally, when I am eating with someone, male or female, for the first time, I notice the details of his or her performance, since it tells a lot about the person, but that time I didn't because the way she took a bite, or chewed, or swallowed, or licked her lips, had no bearing on the fix she was in. I did observe that there was nothing wrong with her appetite, and she proved that she liked the egg-and-anchovy combo by taking her full share. She asked if it was on Nero Wolfe's list of favorites, and I said no, he would probably sneer at it. When the platter was empty she said she hadn't thought it would make her hungry, telling someone the secret she had kept bottled up so long, but it had. She gave me a little smile, the dimples coming, and said, "We don't really know ourselves, do we?"

"It depends," I said. "Some of us know too much, and some not enough. I don't want to know why I get out of bed mornings in a fog, I might never sleep again. To hell with it, I always find my way out. As for you, you're not in a fog, you're under a spotlight that you turned on yourself. Why don't you just turn it off?"

"I did *not* turn it on myself. Other people did it, especially my mother. I *can't* turn it off."

"Well, then. What's your biggest question? Your mother's real name and so on, or your father?"

"My father, of course. After all, I have lived with my mother all my life, and I suppose my wanting to know her real name and things about her is just . . . well, curiosity. But I *must* know about my father. Is he alive? Who is he? What is he? His genes made me!"

I nodded. "Yeah, you went to Smith. You learned too much about genes. Mr. Wolfe said once that scientists should keep their findings strictly to themselves; by spilling it they just complicate things for other people. Would you like some coffee?"

"No, thanks."

"They have good sweet things."

She shook her head. "I admit I could eat anything, it's really amazing, my being so hungry, but I'd rather not. What do you . . . ? You said you might have a suggestion."

"I know I did." I turned a hand over on the table. "You've got a tough one. I'm afraid you need more than a suggestion, even from the one man you can trust. Sure, I filed that. To get what you want—there's one chance in a million that a week or so of poking around would crack it, but it would probably be a long and very expensive job. How much money have you got?"

"Not much. Of course I would want to pay you."

"Not me. I explained that. But Nero Wolfe has inflated ideas about fees; that's why I would have to know exactly how you are fixed. If you care to tell me."

"Certainly I'll tell you. I have never earned any money, not enough to mention, and anyway I've spent it. I only have what my mother left, after paying the . . . for the cremation. She left instructions about that. There's a little more than two thousand dollars in the bank, that's all. There are no debts and I don't owe anyone anything."

I had a brow up. "What did your mother do for—no, that's immaterial. She made enough to send you to an expensive college. Unless someone helped?"

"No. She did it all. You were going to ask what she did for a living. She was with a television producer, the same one from as far back as I can remember. I suppose she got fifteen thousand a year, maybe more. She never told me." The quick brown eyes were straight at me. "If I paid Nero Wolfe the two thousand dollars he would have you work on it, wouldn't he?"

I shook my head. "He wouldn't even discuss it. He would know it might take a year, and he thinks nothing of billing a client five grand for a one-week job. You said you know about him, but apparently you don't. He's pig-headed and high-nosed and toplofty, and he thinks he's the best detective in the world, and so do I, or I would have moved out long ago. I think you deserve some help with your problem, and you certainly need it, and I like your dimples, but if I told him about you and suggested an appointment he would just glare at me. He would think I had a hinge loose. I do have one idea that you might want to consider. Miss Rowan likes to do things for people, and she has a stack, and if you—"

"Don't you dare tell her about me!"

"Keep your seat. I wouldn't dream of telling her, or anyone. I merely thought you might tell her yourself, and—"

"I wouldn't tell *anybody!*"

"Okay, I won't either. Your eyes have a fine flash." I regarded her. "Look, Miss Denovo. I'm shutting the door only because I have to. Myself, I would like to tackle it because it would probably have some interesting angles and twists and it would be nice to have a client it is a pleasure to look at. Besides, there would be the possibility of having to deal with a murder. When you hear about—"

"Murder?"

"Certainly. It's only a bare possibility, but it popped up because when you hear of a hit-and-run death and the driver hasn't been tagged, it does pop up. I mention it only because it's one of the reasons why I would like to tackle it. But there's not a sliver of a chance with Mr. Wolfe, and there you are. I'm sorry, I really am."

She shook her head, with her eyes staying at me. "But Mr. Goodwin. This leaves me helpless." Apparently the murder possibility hadn't fazed her. "What can I do? I can't tell somebody else."

That was that. I wasn't feeling particularly cocky twenty minutes later, as I flagged a taxi headed downtown on Park Avenue and gave the hackie Saul Panzer's address. Working for and with the best detective in the world—which you don't have to swallow—is fine, but when you have been told by a pretty girl that you are the one man in the world she can trust, even if it was pure soap, and you have stiff-armed her, you are not on your high horse. I slouched in the taxi and tried to steer my mind back to baseball and the Mets.

It was six minutes to eight when I got out at the corner of Thirty-eighth and Park. As for what happened to my friends' welfare, not to mention mine, I'll skip it. Sometimes the cards simply will not cooperate.

2

For Friday's program I merely had to follow the script. At a quarter to ten I let myself out of the old brownstone on West Thirty-fifth Street, went to the garage around the corner on Tenth Avenue for the Heron sedan, which Wolfe owns and I drive, and headed for Long Island, where he had been spending three days as the guest of Lewis Hewitt, who has ten thousand orchids in two 100-foot greenhouses. Driving back to Manhattan, with him in back keeping a hold on the installed-on-order strap as usual because, according to him, no automobile can be trusted for a second, I had to be careful about bumps and jerks. Not on account of Wolfe, since I had a theory that jostles were good for him, but because of the pots of orchid plants in the trunk, which were not crated, and two of them were new Laelia crosses of schroederi and ash-worthiana. They were worth maybe a couple of grand, but the important point was that nobody in the world but Hewitt and now Wolfe had any. As I pulled to the curb in front of the old brownstone I blew the horn, and Theodore Horstmann came out and down, as arranged, and helped me take the pots in and up in the elevator to the plant rooms on the roof. Wolfe took his bag himself. On that I have not a theory but a rule. He needs the exercise. By the time I got down to the office he was behind his desk, in the only chair he considers satisfactory for his weight and spread, looking through the accumulated mail, and Fritz came right behind me to announce lunch.

At table, in the dining room across the hall, business talk was out, as always, and anyway there was no business

8

to discuss, and I had no intention of mentioning Amy Denovo's problem, then or ever. The talk may be of anything and everything, usually of Wolfe's choosing, but that time I started it by remarking, as I helped myself from the silver platter, that a man had told me that shish kebab was just as good or better if it was kid instead of lamb. Wolfe said that any dish was better with kid instead of lamb, but that fresh kid, properly butchered and handled, was unattainable in the metropolitan area. Then he switched from meat to words and said it was miscalled shish kebab. It should be seekh kebab. He spelled it. That was what it was called in India, where it originated. In Hindi or Urdu a seekh is a thin iron rod with a loop at one end and a point at the other, and a kebab is a meatball. Some occidental jackass, he said, had made it shish instead of seekh, and it would serve him right if the only seekh kebab he ever got was old tough donkey instead of lamb. He was still commenting on people who garble foreign words when we finished the raspberries, stirred into a mixture, made by Fritz in a double boiler, of cream and sugar and egg yolks and sherry and almond extract, and went across to the office, where he got at his desk with the mail, and I got at mine with the plant records to enter the items he had talked Lewis Hewitt out of.

At four o'clock, when he took the elevator to the roof for his regular two-hour afternoon session with Theodore and the orchids, I took the stairs for the two flights to my room to do some little personal chores, like inspecting socks and changing the ribbon on my personal typewriter. Those operations always take longer than you expect, and when I heard the doorbell, which has a connection to my room, and glanced at my wrist, I was surprised to see that it was twenty to six. I left it to Fritz, who goes when I am not downstairs, but in a couple of minutes the house phone buzzed, and when I got it Fritz said that a young woman who said her name was Denovo wanted to see me, and I asked him to put her in the front room.

When, after mounting the stoop of the old brownstone, you enter, the second door down the hall on your left is the office. The first is to what we call the front room, which isn't used much, mostly for parking people who aren't wanted in the office. Its furniture is nothing much, not like the office or the kitchen, because Wolfe is seldom in it and doesn't give a damn. When I entered, Amy Denovo was on a chair by a window. She stood up and said, "Well, here I am."

"So I see." I crossed to her. "It's nice to see you and I don't want to be rude, but I thought I made it clear yesterday."

"Oh, you made it clear enough." She started a smile but it didn't quite come. "But I decided I had to see you again, and see Nero Wolfe, I suppose, and so I . . . I did something." She had her bag, brown leather with a big clasp, under her left arm. She sat down and opened it, and took out a parcel wrapped in newspaper with rubber bands around it. She held it out and I took it, not wanting to be rude. "That's twenty thousand dollars," she said, "in hundred-dollar bills." Now the smile came. "You would call it twenty grand. Of course you'll want to count it."

No suitable words seemed to be ready for the tongue, so I gave them time by removing the rubber bands and unfolding the newspaper for a look. It was centuries, some new and some used, in batches fastened with paper clips, and they looked real when I flipped through some. There were ten in the batch I counted, and there were twenty batches. I rewrapped them in the newspaper and replaced the rubber bands.

"At five grand a week," she said, "that's enough for four weeks anyway."

From the hall the sound came of the elevator rattling to a stop. Wolfe was down from the plant rooms.

"The five grand was just the fee," I said. "It didn't include expenses. But that was a little special, it isn't always five grand a week. Are you telling me that you want to hire Nero Wolfe and you offer this as a retainer?"

"Yes. Certainly. Provided you're in charge."

"He's always in charge. I merely do the work."

"All right, if you do the work."

"I will. He only does the thinking. I'll explain it to him and then call you in. If you'll wait here?"

She frowned and shook her head. "I don't want to talk about it to anybody but you."

"Then it's out. He wouldn't take a client he hasn't seen. He never has and he never will."

She pressed her lips tight and took a couple of breaths, and finally said, "I guess I can. All right."

"Good. You won't cotton to him, but you can trust him as far as me." I tapped the package. "Do you want to tell me anything about this?"

"No, I don't. There's nothing to tell except there it is."

"I can assume it's in your possession legally?"

"Of course." She was still frowning. "I didn't rob a bank."

"It's still in your possession until he takes the job." I handed her the parcel. "It may take me five minutes or it could be half an hour. If you get tired waiting, there are magazines on the table." I started for the connecting door to the office but decided to go around, and went to the door to the hall instead.

Wolfe was at his desk with his current book, *Incredible Victory*, by Walter Lord. He probably hadn't got much reading in at Hewitt's and would have to catch up. I went to my desk, sat facing him, and waited for him to finish a paragraph. It must have been a long one. He looked up and growled. "Something?"

"Somebody," I said. "A girl in the front room named Amy Denovo. I believe I mentioned a while back that Miss Rowan was collecting material for a book about her father, and she hired this girl to help, and I met her there last week. As I was leaving there yesterday afternoon she —the girl—stopped me down in the lobby and we went to a place and had egg-and-anchovy sandwiches which I have told Fritz about but he wasn't interested. She wanted me to do a job for her because I am the one man in the world she can trust, and I told her I couldn't because I already had a job, and she said then she would hire you if I would do the work, and I explained that I always do the work. Of course the next question, my question, was about money, and I asked it. She said she had two thousand dollars in the bank, left to her by her mother, and that's all. No other resources and no prospects. Since the job would be complicated and might take months and no telling what expenses, I told her nothing doing, I wouldn't even mention it to you. I was sorry because—"

"Pfui." He grunted. "Why do you mention it now?"

"I'll finish the sentence. I was sorry because the job

would probably be interesting, and tough, and it has none
of the aspects that you won't touch. I mention it now
because she is in the front room with a package wrapped
in newspaper containing two hundred hundred-dollar-bills,
twenty thousand dollars, which she wants you to take as a
retainer."

"Where did she get it?"

"I don't know. She says it's in her possession legally."

He put his bookmark, a thin strip of gold that was a
gift from a client, at his page and put the book down.
"What was said yesterday. In full."

I had expected that. He hates to take on a job; anything to hold off a commitment. Also, there was the chance
that there might be one or more details that he could find
unacceptable. I reported. It had taken a lot of practice to
get to where I could give a long conversation verbatim,
but it was a cinch now, even with three or four talking.
As usual, he leaned back and closed his eyes, and didn't
interrupt. There was no reaction even to the "pigheaded
and high-nosed and toplofty." I omitted nothing except
the irrelevant chatter while we were eating. When I finished he stayed put for a minute and then opened his
eyes and straightened up.

He regarded me. "That's not like you, Archie. It's hard-
ly even a sketch. Barely a start."

"Certainly. There was no point in going deeper with a
poor little poor girl."

He looked up at the wall clock and back at me. "You
could have—no matter. Very well. Bring her."

I went and opened the connecting door. She was still in
the chair by the window, and hadn't returned the parcel
to her bag; it was in her lap. I told her to come.

Wolfe seldom rises when someone enters the office, and
never if it's a woman. His expression is always the same
if it's a woman, no matter who or what she is; he is
concentrating on not making a face. There is no telling
what he notices or doesn't; for instance, whether he noticed that the skirt of Amy Denovo's brown-striped summer dress wasn't really a mini; it was only about two
inches above her knees. Certainly he didn't notice that the
knees were worthy of notice, though they were, since that
had no bearing on her acceptability as a client. The seat

of the red leather chair near the end of his desk was too deep for her to settle back, so she sat on the front half, straight, and put her bag on the stand at her elbow, with the parcel in her lap.

Wolfe, his chair swiveled to face her, his fingers curled over the arm ends, spoke. "So Mr. Goodwin impressed you at first sight."

Her eyes, meeting his, widened a little. "Yes. He did."

"That may be a point for you and it may not. It is nothing new for him to impress a young woman. He has reported his conversation with you yesterday, to its conclusion. He says that you now have in your possession, you say legally, twenty thousand dollars in cash, and you offer it to me as retainer for the job you want me to do. Is that correct?"

"Yes, if Mr. Goodwin does the work."

"He would do his share, directed by me except when urgency forbids. The money is in that parcel? May I see it?"

She got up and handed it to him and returned to the chair. He removed the rubber bands and wrapping and took a look at each batch, all twenty of them, stacking them neatly on his desk. He turned to me. "I see no indication of source. Did you?"

I said no.

He turned to her. "Did Miss Lily Rowan supply it?"

"Of course not!"

"But of course someone did. In view of what you told Mr. Goodwin yesterday, I would have to know the source of this money. Where and how did you get it?"

Her lips were tight. She opened them to say, "I don't see why you have to know that. There's nothing wrong with the way I got it. It's mine. If I went to a store to buy something and gave them one of those bills they wouldn't ask me where I got it."

He shook his head. "Not a parallel, Miss Denovo. Yesterday you told Mr. Goodwin that two thousand dollars in the bank was all you had, and you rejected his suggestion that you ask Miss Rowan to help you." He tapped the stack. "This is ten times two thousand. If it was a loan or a gift I would have to know from whom. If you sold something I would have to know what you sold and to whom. You may not know, at your age, that that is merely reasonable prudence. To accept a substantial retainer for a difficult and complicated operation without assurance of its legitimacy would be asinine, and if you won't tell me where you got this money I won't take it. If you do tell me it will have to be verified, with proper discretion, but to my satisfaction."

She was frowning again, not at him, at me, but it wasn't really for me; it was for the problem she had been handed. But when she spoke it was to me and for me, a question: "Is he right, Mr. Goodwin? Or is he just shutting the door, as you did?"

"No," I said, "I'm afraid he's right. As he said, just reasonable prudence. And after all, if it's yours legally, as you told me, and if there's nothing wrong with the way you got it, as you told him, why not spill it? It can't be a deeper secret than the one we already know."

She looked at Wolfe and back at me. "I could tell *you*," she said.

"Okay, tell me, and we'll pretend he's not here."

"I guess I was being silly." Her eyes were meeting mine. "After what you already know, you might as well know this too. That money came from my father. That and a lot more."

Both of my brows went up. "That makes a liar of you yesterday. Yesterday you had never had your father and didn't know who or what he was, and the two thousand—"

"I know. That was true, I never had a father. This is what happened. When my mother died I came to New York, of course, but I had to go back for graduation, and anyway Mr. Thorne had her instructions, about cremation, and that there was to be no funeral, and he attended to all the . . . the details. Then when I came to New York after the graduation he came—"

"Mr. Thorne?"

"Yes. He came—"

"Who is he?"

"He's the television producer my mother worked for. He came to see me, to the apartment, and he brought things—papers and bills and letters and other things from my mother's desk in her room at the office. And a box, a locked metal box with a label glued on it that said

Property of Amy Denovo. And a key with a tag that said *Key to Amy Denovo's box.* It had been—"

"Was your mother's name Amy?"

"No, her name was Elinor. The key had been in a locked drawer in her desk. The box had been in the office safe. It had been there for years—at least fifteen years, Mr. Thorne said. It's about this long." She held her opened hands about sixteen inches apart. "I waited until he had gone to open it, and I was glad I did. There were just two things in it: money, hundred-dollar bills—the box was more than half full—and a sealed envelope with my name on it. I opened the envelope and it was a letter from my mother, not a long one, just one page. You want to know what it said."

"I sure do. Have you got it?"

"Not here, it's at home, but I know it by heart. It's on her personal letterhead. It isn't dated. It says: *Dear Amy, This money is from your father. I have not seen him or heard from him since four months before you were born but two weeks after you were born I received a bank check for one thousand dollars in the mail, and I have received one every month since then, and it now amounts to exactly one hundred thousand dollars. I don't know what it will be when you read this. I didn't ask for it and I don't want it. I want nothing from your father. You are my daughter, and I can feed you and clothe you and give you a place to live, and I will. And see that you are properly educated. But this money came from your father, so it belongs to you, and here it is. I could put it in a bank to draw interest, but there would be taxes to pay and records of it, so I do it this way. Your mother.* And below *Your mother* she signed her name, Elinor Denovo —only I don't think that was her name. And it must have kept coming right up to the time she died, because it's two hundred and sixty-four thousand dollars. Of course I can't put it in a bank or anything like that because I would have to tell how I got it. Wouldn't I? And I won't."

I looked at Wolfe. He was looking, not at her or at me, but at the stack of lettuce on his desk. Another man could have been thinking that life certainly plays cute tricks, but he was probably reflecting that that was just one-thir-

teenth of what a father had paid for the privilege, or
something similar.

I said, to him, "So it wasn't a loan or a gift and she
didn't sell anything, but we'll have to concede that it's
legally in her possession. Of course the Internal Revenue
Service and the New York State Income Tax Bureau
would like to take a whack at it, but that's not our lookout and what they don't know won't hurt her. What else
shall I ask her?"

He grunted and turned to her. "Is the money still in
the box?"

"Yes, all but that." She gestured toward his desk. "The
box is in my apartment—on Eighty-second Street. And the
letter. But I don't want . . . Mr. Goodwin mentioned the
Internal Revenue Service."

"We are not government agents, Miss Denovo, and are
not obliged to disclose information received in confidence."
He swiveled his head to look at the clock. "It is ten
minutes to our dinnertime. May Mr. Goodwin call on you
at your apartment at ten tomorrow morning?"

"Yes. I don't go to Miss Rowan on Saturday."

"Then expect him around ten o'clock. He will want to
see the box and its contents, and the letter, and he will
want all the information you can give him. What you told
him yesterday is a mere prologue." He turned. "Archie.
Give her a receipt for this money. Not as a retainer; that
can wait until you have seen the box and the letter,
and you will verify the handwriting of the letter. Just a
receipt for the amount, her property, entrusted to me for
safekeeping."

I turned my chair, pulled the typewriter around, and
opened a drawer for paper and carbon.

3

I was interested, naturally, in Elinor Denovo's apartment. We were probably going to need to know everything about her that was knowable, and a woman's home can have a hundred hints, two or three of which you may get if you have any savvy at all and are lucky. So before settling down with Amy and my notebook in the living room I took a tour, with Amy along. There were a small foyer, a medium-sized living room, two bedrooms, a bathroom, and a small kitchen. If the foyer or kitchen or bathroom had any hints they weren't for me; for instance, there was nothing in the bathroom to indicate that it had ever been used by a man, but of course Elinor hadn't been there for nearly three months.

I gave Amy's bedroom just a glance; for her I had a better source of hints, herself. She said she hadn't changed anything in her mother's bedroom. It might have told a woman, especially a Lily Rowan, a lot, but all I got was that she had liked pale green for drapes and the bed cover, she used three different scents, all expensive, and she didn't mind if the rug had a big spot near the bathroom door. The living room did have a few hints which might help or might not. There were five pictures on the walls, and they were all color reproductions of paintings by Georgia O'Keeffe—data supplied by Amy. I would have to check on O'Keeffe. The only piece of furniture that was upholstered was the couch, and there were only two cushions on it. I have seen couches with a dozen. The four chairs didn't match one another, and none of them matched the couch. The books, seven whole shelves of them, were such a mixture, all kinds, fiction and non-fiction, that after I had looked at twenty or thirty titles I quit.

The one really good hint, if someone would tell me what it meant, was that there were no photographs. Except for those in Amy's room, which belonged to her, there wasn't a single photograph in the place, not one, of any-one or anything. That was hard to believe, but Amy said that as far as she knew there had never been any, and she had none of her mother, not even a snapshot, which was a setback, since we would certainly want to know what Elinor Denovo had looked like. I would probably have had to look long and far to find another middle-aged woman who had died, or would die, absolutely photo-graphless.

There were papers, letters, and paid bills and miscel-laneous items, including the stuff from her room at the office, but there was no diary or anything resembling one, and there was nothing that seemed likely to be of any help. If it got too tough I might have to have another go at it or put Saul Panzer on it. I did use a few of the items, in Elinor's handwriting, to check the writing on the letter that was in the box with the money. It geed.

When I finally sat on the couch with my notebook, with Amy on one side and the box on the other, it was getting on toward noon. Amy looked two years younger; she hadn't bunched her hair and it was dancing around when she moved her head. I got a piece of folded paper from my breast pocket.

"Here's a receipt," I said, "signed by Mr. Wolfe, which he told me to give you if the box and its contents checked, and I admit they do. You are now a client in good stand-ing." I handed it to her. "Now a suggestion. We discussed you after dinner last evening. You have been damned lucky; a closet shelf is no place for a quarter of a million dollars' worth of skins. If you get the thought that what we're concerned about is the fact that some of it may be needed for the job if it drags on, that's all right, but it's also a fact that we're concerned with a client's interests from every angle, not just the job. So we have a sugges-tion. Banks are closed today and tomorrow. When I leave I'll take the box along and put it in the safe in our office. Monday morning I'll take it to your bank and meet you there. Which bank is it?"

"The Continental. The Eighty-sixth Street branch."

"That's fine. Mr. Wolfe's is the Thirty-fourth Street branch and so is mine. We'll get twelve bank checks for twenty grand each, payable to you, and I'll have with me letters to twelve different savings banks in New York, ready for your signature, opening savings accounts. You'll endorse the bank checks and we'll enclose them in the letters. The interest will come to a thousand dollars a month, which is a nice coincidence. You'll deposit the remaining four grand in your account at the Continental."

She was frowning. "But . . . what will happen? How will I explain . . . ?"

"You won't have to explain anything. If at some time in the future the Internal Revenue Service gets nosy and tries to hook you, you owe them nothing because it was gifts from your father, stretched out over twenty-two years, and Mr. Wolfe is sure that they'll have to lump it, and so am I. They couldn't claim it was used for your support because it wasn't, not a cent of it. If you stash it in a safe-deposit box and peel off twelve grand a year, it will last twenty years. If you do what we suggest, you'll get twelve grand a year and there will be no peeling off. And of course you could withdraw it any time and buy race horses or something."

She gave me a smile. "I'd like to think about it a little. I knew I could trust you. I'll decide before you go."

"Good. A question. Have there been any bank checks in the mail for your mother since she died? Either here or at the office?"

"No, not here. If there had been any at the office of course Mr. Thorne would have told me."

"Okay. I should mention that I no longer think it may take a year. A week may do it, or even less. Your mother made a mistake in that letter. If she didn't want you to find out who your father was, and obviously she didn't, she shouldn't have mentioned that it came in bank checks. There was and is a trail, there has to be, between those checks and the sender, and she probably cashed them at a bank, since they're centuries. Ten centuries every month. It must have been a bank, and probably her bank. We'll find out Monday." I opened my notebook. "Now for questions, and some of them will be very personal."

That took a full hour, and I barely made it home by lunchtime. Wolfe was standing in the doorway to the dining room when I entered. By standing there he was asking me, without putting it into words, why I hadn't phoned that I might be late, but since I was only three minutes late I ignored it and merely asked him if he wanted to take a glance inside the box before lunch. He said no, and I took it to the office and put it on his desk and then went and joined him at the table. As I sat I said it wouldn't hurt his appetite to know that she had taken our suggestion and would meet me at her bank Monday morning, so if more than the retainer was needed it would be available.

As a rule we stay at the table for coffee at lunch, though not at dinner, but sometimes, when I have or may have something to report about a job he is committed to, he tells Fritz to bring it to the office, and my bringing the box showed that he was committed. So when we had put away the diced watermelon, which had been sprinkled with granulated sugar and refrigerated in a cup of sherry for an hour, we moved across the hall and Fritz brought coffee. I opened the box, but he merely gave it a brief glance and sat, and I went to my desk, swung my chair around, and got my notebook from a pocket.

"I was there nearly three hours," I said. "Do you want the crop?"

"No." He was pouring coffee. "Only what may be useful."

"Then you should be back at your book in about ten minutes. To simplify it I'll make it Elinor and Amy. The most interesting item is the fact that Elinor had no photographs anywhere, not even at the bottom of a drawer. Not one. That's extremely significant, so please tell me what it signifies."

He made a noise, not enough of one to be called a grunt. "Did you get nothing at all?" He sipped coffee.

"Close to it. The trouble is, Amy doesn't know anything. I doubt if there's another girl anywhere who had a mother for twenty-two years and knows so little about her. One thing she knows, or thinks she does, is that her mother hated her and tried hard to hide it. She says that Amy means 'beloved,' and that Elinor probably wasn't aware that she was being sarcastic when she named her that."

I went to the pot of coffee on Wolfe's desk, poured a full cup, returned to my chair, and took a couple of sips. "Did Elinor have any close friends, men or women? Amy doesn't know. Of course she has been away at college for most of the last four years. What was Elinor's basic character? Careful, correct, and cold about covers it, according to Amy. One of the words she used was 'introvert,' which I would have supposed was moth-eaten for a girl just out of Smith."

I flipped a page of my notebook. "Elinor must have dropped some hints without thinking, at least one little one in twenty years, about her background, her childhood, but Amy says no. She doesn't know what Elinor did for a living before she went to work for Raymond Thorne Productions, the firm she was with when she died. She doesn't even know what Elinor did, specifically, at Thorne's; she only knows it must have been an important job."

I flipped another page and took some coffee. "Believe it or not, Amy doesn't know where she was born. She thinks it might have been Mount Sinai Hospital, because that's where Elinor went for an appendectomy about ten years ago, but that's just a guess. Anyway it probably wouldn't help much, since Elinor certainly wasn't letting things she didn't want known get into the record. Amy does know one thing, and of course it's essential, the date. She was born April twelfth, nineteen forty-five. About five years ago she decided to see the doctor who signed her birth certificate but found he was dead. So she was conceived around the middle of July nineteen forty-four, so that's the time to place Elinor, but Amy doesn't know where she was living. The first home Amy remembers was a walkup, two flights, on West Ninety-second Street, when she was three. When she was seven they moved to a better one on West Seventy-eighth Street, and when she was thirteen they jumped the park to the East Side, to the one I inspected this morning."

I emptied my cup and decided it was enough. "I'll skip the details of the inspection unless you insist. As I said, no photographs, which is fantastic. The letters and other papers, a washout. If we fed them to a computer I would expect it to come up with something like SO WHAT or TELL IT TO THE MARINES. It would have been a pleasure to find for instance a newspaper clipping about a man, no matter what it said, but nothing doing. Did I mention that Amy has no photograph of her mother? We'll have to snare one somehow." I shut the notebook and tossed it on the desk. "Questions?"

He said, "Grrrhh."

"I agree. Oh, you asked me last evening if Amy is interested not so much in genes but in gold. Does she think that a father who could be so free with bank checks must have a barrel of it and she would like to dip in? I passed, and I still do. After spending three hours with her I doubt it, and anyway, does it matter? To us?"

"No." He put his cup down and pushed it back. "Monday should be more fruitful. You're off, I suppose."

I nodded. "I was expected last evening, as you know." I rose. "Shall I put that in the safe?"

He said no, he would, and I gave him the key to the box, put the notebook in a drawer, whirled my chair and pushed it against my desk as always, and went—out and up to my room to change and pack a bag. I had phoned Lily that I would make it in time for dinner.

It was a quarter to three when I left the house, walked around the corner to the garage, got the Heron, and headed up Tenth Avenue. At Thirty-sixth Street I turned right. The direct route would have been left on Forty-fifth Street for the West Side Highway, but I don't like to have something itching me when I'm stretched out at the edge of Lily's swimming pool and flowers are smelling and birds are flying and so on. On East Forty-third Street parking was no problem on Saturday afternoon.

Entering the *Gazette* building, I took the elevator to the twentieth floor. For the file I could have gone to the morgue instead, but Lon Cohen might know of some recent development that the *Gazette* hadn't had room for. When I entered his room, two doors down from the publisher's corner room, he was talking to one of the three phones on his desk and I sat on the one other chair, at the end of the desk, and waited. When he hung up he swung around and said, "After what happened Thursday night how did you get here? Walk? You sure didn't have taxi fare."

I answered suitably, and when personal comments were, in my opinion, even, I said I knew I shouldn't bother an assistant to a publisher about something trivial; I only wanted to get the details of a hit-and-run that had killed a woman named Elinor Denovo, the last week in May, and would he ring the morgue and tell them to oblige me. He got at a phone and did what he knew I expected him to, told someone to bring the file up to him. When a boy came with it, in about six minutes, no more, he was at another phone and I had moved my chair about a foot back to be discreet. The boy put the file on his desk and I reached and got it.

There were only seven items: four clippings and three typed reports. It hadn't made the front page, but was on page 3 for Saturday, May 27, and the first thing I noticed was that there was no picture of her, so even the *Gazette* hadn't dug one up. I went through everything. Mrs. Elinor Denovo (so she was Mrs. to the world) had returned her car to the garage where she kept it, on Second Avenue near Eighty-third Street, Friday night after midnight, and told the attendant she would want it around noon the next day. Three minutes later, as she was crossing Eighty-third Street in the middle of the block, presumably bound for her apartment on Eighty-second Street, a car had hit her, tossed her straight ahead, and run over her with two wheels. Only four people had seen it happen: a man on the sidewalk walking east, a hundred feet or more away, a man and woman on the sidewalk going west, the same direction as the car, about the same distance away, and a taxi driver who had just turned his cab into Eighty-third Street from Second Avenue. They all said that the car that hit her hadn't even slowed down, but were unanimous on nothing else. The hackie thought the driver, alone in the car, was a woman. The man coming east said it was a man, alone. The man and woman thought it was two men, both in the front seat. The hackie thought the car was a Dodge Coronet but wasn't sure; the man coming east said it was a Chevvy; the man and woman didn't know. Two of them said the car was dark green, one said it was dark blue, and one said it was black. So much for eyewitnesses. Actually, it was a dark-gray Ford. It was hot. Mrs. David A. Ernst of Scarsdale, who owned it, had gone for it at ten o'clock Friday evening where she had parked it on West Eleventh Street, and it wasn't there. A cop had spotted it Saturday afternoon parked on East 123rd Street, and by Monday the scientists had cinched it that it was the one that had got Elinor Denovo.

By the time the *Gazette* went to press on Thursday, June first, the date of the last clipping, the police had got nowhere. They didn't even claim that anyone had been invited in for questioning, let alone name a suspect; they only said that the investigation was being vigorously pursued, which was probably true, since they hate a hit-and-run and don't quit until it's absolutely hopeless, and even then they don't forget it.

There was nothing about Elinor Denovo that I didn't already know, except that she was vice-president of Raymond Thorne Productions, Inc. Miss Amy Denovo had been interviewed but hadn't said much. Raymond Thorne had said that Mrs. Denovo had made valuable contributions to the art of television production and her death was a great loss not only for his company but for the whole television industry and therefore for the country. I thought he should make up his mind whether television was an art or an industry.

I put the file on Lon's desk, waited until he had finished at a phone, and said, "Many thanks. I was curious about a detail. The latest item is June first. Would you know if there has been any progress since?"

He got at a phone, the green one this time, pressed a button, and in a moment talked, and then waited. While he waited another phone buzzed, and stopped when he pushed a button. In a couple of minutes he told the green phone, "Yeah, sure." In another couple of minutes he cradled it, turned to me and said, "Apparently it's dead. Our last word, more than a month ago, was that we might as well cross it off. They had only one man still on it. But now of course, with Nero Wolfe horning in, it's far from dead. So it was murder. I don't expect you to name him, even off the record, but I want enough for a page one box."

I was on my feet. "Journalists," I said, "are the salt and pepper of the earth. I would enjoy discussing that with you, but I'm on my way to a rustic swimming pool in the middle of a tailor-made glade in the Westchester woods, and I'm twenty hours late. I said it was something trivial, but have it your way. Yes, it was murder, and the driver of the car was the skunk who topped my three aces with four deuces Thursday night. I hope they get him."

I turned and went.

But down in the lobby I went to a phone booth, dialed a number I didn't have to look up, gave my name, asked if Sergeant Stebbins was around, and after a long wait got his voice:

"Stebbins. Something up, Archie?"

He must have just won a bet or got a raise. He called me Archie only about once in two years, and sometimes he wouldn't even say Goodwin but made it just *you*. I returned the compliment. "Nothing with a bite, Purley, just a routine question, but to answer it you may have to look at a file. You may have forgotten it, it was nearly three months ago—a hit-and-run on East Eighty-third Street, a woman named Elinor Denovo—"

"We haven't forgotten it. We don't forget a hit-and-run."

"I know you don't, I was just being impolite for practice. Someone asked me if you've dug up a lead on it, and of course I didn't know. Have you?"

"Who asked you?"

"Oh, Mr. Wolfe and I were discussing crime and whether cops are as good as they ought to be, and he mentioned this Elinor Denovo. As you know, he misses nothing in the papers. I said you would probably get that one, and I was curious. Of course I'm not asking for any inside dope . . ."

"There isn't any dope, inside or outside. It's hanging. But we're not forgetting it."

"Right. I hope you get him. Nobody likes a hit-and-run."

Walking to Forty-third Street for the car, I had to concede that I had got no relief at all for the itch.

4

You would suppose that at ten minutes to ten Monday morning, as I sat in a taxicab headed uptown, with the box on the seat beside me and the breast pocket of my jacket bulging with envelopes containing letters to twelve savings banks because I never lug a brief case if I can help it, my mind would be on the morning's program, but it wasn't. It was on the hour just past, or part of it, instead of the one just ahead. I don't like to have people bellow at me, particularly not Wolfe.

Also I had had only six hours' sleep, a full two hours less than I need and nearly always get. Getting home after midnight Sunday, I had decided against typing twelve letters before turning in, and so had to set the alarm for seven o'clock. When it went off I opened one eye to glare at it, but I knew I would have to hustle, much as I hate hustling before breakfast, and in six minutes, maybe seven, I was on my feet. At 7:45 I was at the little table in the kitchen where I eat breakfast, on the last swallow of orange juice, and Fritz was crossing to me with the grilled ham and corn fritters, and at 8:10 I was in the office at the typewriter. At 9:15 I had finished the twelfth letter and had started folding and putting them in envelopes when the doorbell rang, and I went to the hall for a look through the one-way glass in the front door, and saw a big burly male with a big round red face topped by a big battered broad-brimmed felt hat. The hat alone would have been enough. Inspector Cramer of Homicide South must be the only man in New York who wears such a hat on a hot sunny day in August.

Nuts, I thought, let him ring. But it must be just for

26

me, since he knew Wolfe was never available before eleven o'clock, so I went and opened the door and said, "Good morning and greetings, but I'm busy and I'm in a rush. I really mean it."

"So am I." It was gruff, but it always is. "I'm just stopping by on my way down. Why did you call Stebbins on that hit-and-run?"

"What the hell, I told him why."

"I know you did. Also I know you and I know Wolfe. Discussing crime my ass. All right, discuss it with me now. I want to know why you're working on that hit-and-run."

"I'm not. Mr. Wolfe isn't." I glanced at my wrist. "I would like to ask you in for some give and take, you know I enjoy that, but I've got a date. Except for what was in the papers, I know absolutely nothing about that hit-and-run, and neither does Mr. Wolfe. No one has consulted with us about it. The only client we've got is a girl who can't find her father and wants us to." I glanced at my wrist. "Damn it, I'll be late." I started the door around. He opened his mouth, clamped it shut, about-faced, and started down the seven steps of the stoop. His PD car was there, double-parked. By the time he reached it I was back in the office.

Time was short, but it was quite possible that Cramer would phone while I was gone, and Wolfe didn't know about my call to Purley Stebbins. He is not to be disturbed short of an emergency when he is up in the plant rooms, but he had to be told, so I took the house phone and pushed a button, and after a wait his voice came.

"Yes?"

"Me in a hurry. Cramer was here just now, stopping on his way downtown. I haven't had a chance to tell you that Saturday afternoon I rang Stebbins and—"

"I'm busy!" he bellowed and hung up.

I assumed he had just found a thrip on a favorite plant or dry rot on a pseudobulb, but as I said, I do not like to be bellowed at. If Cramer called they could discuss crime. When the letters were in the envelopes and in my pocket I still had a chore left, ringing Mortimer M. Hotchkiss, the vice-president who bossed the Thirty-fourth Street branch of the Continental Bank and Trust Company. That didn't take long; he was always glad to be of service to a depositor—not me, Nero Wolfe—whose balance never went below five figures and sometimes hit six. That done, I got the box from the safe and was off. Nothing was in it but the money; the letter was on a shelf with some other classified items.

At the Eighty-sixth Street branch I found that Hotchkiss had been prompt. I was only six steps inside when a man at a desk got up and motioned me over and asked if I was Mr. Goodwin, and then took me inside the rail and along an aisle to a door at the front. He opened it and bowed me in, and there was Amy Denovo on a chair facing a big glass-topped desk. Behind the desk was a middle-aged banker with a shiny dome and rimless cheaters. As I crossed he rose and offered a hand, saying that it was a pleasure, Mr. Goodwin, a real pleasure, which was par, since Hotchkiss was a vice-president and he wasn't. I said, "Mr. Atwood?" and he said yes and told me to sit, but after telling Amy good morning I put the box on the desk, fished the key from my pocket and used it, and opened the lid wide. Then I sat. Atwood had started to, but was up again, staring at the contents of the box. It rated a stare, even from a banker.

"That belongs to Miss Denovo," I said. "I assume that Mr. Hotchkiss told you that I work for Nero Wolfe. Miss Denovo has engaged Mr. Wolfe's services, and I'm here for her. That's two hundred and forty-four thousand dollars, all in centuries. Miss Denovo would like to have twelve bank checks for twenty grand each, payable to her, and the remaining four grand deposited in her account."

"Certainly," he said. He looked at her and back at me. "That's quite a . . . quite a . . . certainly. Do you want . . . it will take a while, a little while—counting it and making out the checks."

I nodded. "Sure. Certainly. Anyway, if you're not too busy, we'd like to discuss something with you."

"Cer—I'll be glad to, Mr. Goodwin." His hand started for the phone on the desk, but he changed his mind. He closed the lid of the box, tucked it under his arm, said he would be back soon, and went.

When the door was shut Amy asked, "What's he going to do?"

"His duty," I said. "The slogan of this bank is: THE

BANK YOU CAN BANK ON. You have crossed and uncrossed your ankles three times. Relax."

What "soon" means depends on the circumstances. For there and then I would have supposed about five minutes, but twelve had passed when the door opened and Atwood entered, closed the door, crossed to his desk, and sat. He looked at me, then at her, and back at me, trying to decide which one the bank wanted to bank on it. "It will take a little while," he said. "You wanted to discuss something?"

"Right," I said. "Of course a bank is choosy about handing out information about its customers, but I am speaking for Miss Denovo. Her mother had an account here for nine years. Naturally, when you saw what was in that box you wondered where it came from. We think a lot of it came from your bank."

He gawked at me. A banker shouldn't gawk, but he did. He opened his mouth, shut it, and opened it again to say, "I'll ask you to explain that statement, Mr. Goodwin."

"I'm going to. Every month for twenty-two years Mrs. Elinor Denovo cashed a bank check for a thousand dollars. She always asked for and got it in hundred-dollar bills. That's where the contents of that box came from. She never spent a dollar of it. From your expression I suppose you're thinking this may be leading to something ugly, blackmail for instance, but it isn't. It's perfectly clean. The point is, we have assumed that Mrs. Denovo cashed the checks here, probably a hundred of them in nine years, and her daughter wants to know the name of the bank that drew them. She would also like to know if they were payable to Elinor Denovo, or to cash or bearer."

His eyes went to Amy and he thought he was going to ask her something, but returned to me. His face had cleared some, but he was still a banker and always would be. He spoke. "As you said, Mr. Goodwin, banks are choosy about giving out information regarding their customers. They should be."

"Sure. I wasn't crabbing."

"But since it's for Miss Denovo, and it's about her mother, I'm not going to, uh, hem and haw. I don't have to consult my staff to answer your questions. As a man of wide experience, you probably know that it is considered proper and desirable for a bank official to keep informed about the—well, call it habits, of the customers. I have known about those checks cashed by Mrs. Denovo for several years. One each and every month. They were drawn by the Seaboard Bank and Trust Company, the main office on Broad Street, payable to bearer." He looked at Amy and back at me. "As a matter of fact, I tell you frankly that I'm obliged to you. Any banker, if someone walked in with a quarter of a million dollars in currency, would be . . . well, curious. He should be. You understand that. So I'm glad you told me . . . well, I'm obliged to you. And to you, Miss Denovo." He actually grinned— a real, frank grin. "A bank you can bank on. But that's all I can tell you about those checks because it's all I know."

"It's all we wanted."

"Good." He rose. "I'll see how they're getting on." He went. When the door was shut Amy started to say something, but I shook my head at her. There were probably ten thousand rooms in the five boroughs that were bugged. The office of the top guy at a branch bank might be one of them, and if so that was no place to discuss any part of a secret that the client had kept the lid on for most of her life, or even give a hint. So to pass the time, since it wouldn't be sociable just to sit and stare back at Amy, I got up and went to take a look at the titles of books on shelves at the wall, and when *International Bank Directory* caught my eye I slid it out, opened it at New York, and turned to the page I wanted.

I would have said that the odds were at least a million to one against one of the officers or directors of the Seaboard Bank and Trust Company being someone we had a good line to, and when I saw that name, Avery Ballou, the second one on the alphabetical list of the Board of Directors, I said, "I'll be damned," so loud that Amy twisted around.

"What's the matter?" she asked.

I told her nothing was the matter, just the contrary; we had just got a break I would explain later.

The rest of the errand at the bank was merely routine. At eleven o'clock Amy and I were sitting at a table in a drugstore on Madison Avenue, her with coffee and me with a glass of milk. The twelve letters had been dropped into a mailbox at the corner and the empty box was beside me on a chair. I had told her why I had shushed her at the bank, and about the break, of course not mentioning Ballou's name, and had offered to bet her a finif that we would spot her father within three days, but she said she wouldn't bet against what she wanted. At 11:10 I said I had to make a phone call, went to the booth, dialed the number I knew best, and after eight rings got what I expected.

"Yes?"

He knows darned well that's no way to answer a phone, but try to change him.

"Me," I said. "In a drugstore with the client, having refreshments. The letters have been mailed, with enclosures, and she is taking the box home as a souvenir of her mother or father, I don't know which. Three items. First, what I started to tell you this morning when you bellowed at me. Cramer may phone, so you ought to know that I rang Stebbins Saturday afternoon. I told him that you and I were discussing crime the other day and the hit-and-run that killed a woman named Elinor Denovo came up, and I wondered if they had got a lead. He told Cramer, and of course Cramer thinks that the simplest question from you or me means that we've got something hot. I told him that we only knew what we read in the papers. If he phones, you—"

"Pfui. What else?"

"Second, you said Friday evening that my next stop after the bank would be Raymond Thorne. Any change?"

"No."

"Third, the bank was pie. The checks were drawn by the Seaboard Bank and Trust Company, the third largest bank in town, payable to bearer, and I took a look at it in the *International Bank Directory*. I won't mention his name on the phone, but you remember that one winter evening about a year and a half ago a man sat in the office and said to you, quote, 'I have never spent an hour in a pink bedroom,' end quote. Well, he's on the Board of Directors of the Seaboard Bank and Trust Company."

"Indeed." A five-second pause. "Satisfactory."

"All of that. The kind of break you read about. Shall I take him first instead of Thorne?"

"I think not." Another pause. "It needs reflection."

"Okay. Don't stand in the hall at lunchtime. I may not make it."

When I got back to the table Amy had started her third cup of coffee. As I sat she said, "I've been thinking. You're wonderful, Mr. Goodwin. Simply wonderful. I wish . . . I want to call you Archie."

"Try it and see what happens. I might like it. Since you say your mother was being sarcastic when she tagged you Amy I suppose you wish your name was Araminta or Hephzibah, or you pick it."

"I could pick a better one."

"I'll bet you could. Now we have a problem. I have to ask people questions about your mother, a few of those whose names you gave me yesterday, and I am to start with Raymond Thorne. You'll phone him and tell him you're sending me and you hope he'll cooperate, but I can't just say I'm after men your mother knew in the summer of nineteen forty-four—that's when the genes met —since you don't want anyone to know or even suspect that it's a father hunt. So I have a suggestion, approved by Mr. Wolfe, which we expect you to approve."

"Oh, I'll approve anything you—" She stopped and tightened her lips. Then she smiled. "Listen to me. You might think I had no brains at all. Tell me and we'll see."

I told her.

5

The office of Raymond Thorne Productions was on the sixth floor of one of the newer steel-and-glass hives on Madison Avenue in the Forties. Judging from its size, and the furniture and fixtures, and the cordial smile of the receptionist, the television art, or maybe industry, was doing fine. Also I had to wait twenty minutes to get in to Thorne, though he had told Amy on the phone that his door would always be open for her or anyone she sent.

Of course I wasn't suspecting that he might himself be the target. In her letter Elinor had told Amy that she hadn't seen or heard from her father since four months before she was born, and there was no reason to suppose that that might be flam and she had seen him every work day for twenty years. The idea that a detective should suspect everything that everybody says is a good general rule, but there's a limit.

Thorne and his room went together fine. The room was big and modern and so was he. After giving me a man-to-man handshake and saying how much he would like to help Amy any way he could, and telling me to sit, he returned to his desk and said he didn't know what it was I wanted because Amy had been rather vague on the phone.

I nodded. "She thought I could tell it better, but it's really very simple. She wants Nero Wolfe—you may have heard the name."

"Oh, sure."

"She wants him to find out who killed her mother. I think she's a little hipped on it, but that's her privilege.

She thinks the cops should have nailed him long ago, and also she thinks they went at it wrong. She thinks it was premeditated murder. In fact, she's sure it was. Don't ask me why she's sure; I have asked her, and she says it's intuition. How old were you when you learned not to argue with intuition?"

"It's so long ago I've forgotten."

"Me too. But intuition hasn't told her who it was. She has made a list of names, twenty-eight of them, people who were friends of her mother, everybody who had personal contact that could be called close even by stretching it, and she has said no to all of them. She says none of them could possibly have had a reason, so it must have been someone she doesn't know about—someone connected with her work here, or someone from many years ago when she was too young to remember. Therefore I come to you first, naturally. She worked here, and you knew her—how long?"

"More than twenty years." He had his head cocked. "Do *you* think it was premeditated murder?"

"Mr. Wolfe would say it's 'cogitable.' He likes words like that. It could have been; none of the facts say no. If we find someone with a healthy motive that will make it interesting. The first thing I would like from you is a photograph of Mrs. Denovo. You must have some."

His eyes left me for a quick glance down and to the right, then up again. "I don't think . . ." He let that go. "Didn't you get one from Amy?"

"She hasn't any. There aren't any in the apartment. Surely you have some. At least one."

"Well . . ." He glanced down again. "I'm not surprised that there are none in the apartment. Mrs. Denovo had a thing about photographs—I mean of her. When we wanted pictures of the staff, for promotion, we had to leave her out. She couldn't be persuaded. Once we got up a folder with separate pictures of seven of us, but not of her, though she should have been up front, after me. No picture of her at all, period." He rubbed his chin with fingertips, eying me. "But I've got one."

"Yeah." I gestured with a hand. "There in the bottom drawer."

His head jerked up. "How the hell do you know?"

"Any detective just learning how would have known, and I've been at it for years. When I said 'photograph' you glanced down there; you did it twice."

His head went back to normal. "Well, you're wrong. They're in the *next* to the bottom drawer. Two of them. They were taken years ago by a camera man trying angles, and she didn't know they existed. A week or so after her death I remembered about them and took a look in the old files and found them. But I don't think I should . . . Well, if she had known they were there she would have destroyed them long ago. Wouldn't she?"

"Probably. But she's dead. And if Amy's intuition happens to be right and it was murder, and if the photos would help us get him, do *you* want to destroy them?"

"No. Of course I don't."

"I should hope not. May I see them, please?"

He leaned over to reach down to the drawer, came up with a brown envelope, slipped two prints out, and gave them a look. They were about five by eight inches. "Until I saw these," he said, "I had forgotten how attractive she was. It must have been nineteen forty-six or forty-seven, a year or so after she came here. My God, how people change."

I had got up and circled the end of the desk, and he handed them to me. One was about three-quarters face and the other was profile. There wasn't much of her figure, not down to her waist, but they were good shots of a good face. There was some resemblance to Amy, but the forehead was a little wider and the chin a little more pointed. I looked at the back, but there was no date or other data.

"I can't let you take them," Thorne said, "but I can have copies made. As many as you want."

I gave them another look. "They could be extremely useful. I can have copies made and return these to you."

He said no, they were the only pictures he had of a woman who had been a big help to him for many years, and he was going to hang on to them, and I handed them over. I told him I needed at least six copies, ten would be better, and returned to my chair and got out my notebook.

"Now a leading question," I said. "You'll dodge it, naturally, but I'll ask it anyway. Amy thought it might be someone connected with her work here. Could you suggest a candidate?"

He shook his head. "You mentioned that before. I don't have to dodge. Forget it. There are forty-six people in this organization, counting everybody. Over the years there have been, oh, I suppose around a hundred and fifty. They haven't all thought Mrs. Denovo was perfect, we've had our share of scraps and grudges, but murder? Not a chance. Forget it."

Of course I was glad to, since Amy's father couldn't have been one of the hundred and fifty unless Elinor had lied in the letter, and I decided it wasn't necessary to nag him just to keep up appearances. I opened the notebook. "Okay, we'll pass that for now. Now some dates. When did Mrs. Denovo start with you?"

"I looked that up the day I found the pictures. It was July second, nineteen forty-five."

"You had known her before that?"

"No. She walked in that morning and said she had heard that I needed a stenographer. I was in radio then—we got into television later—and I had only four people in three little rooms on Thirty-ninth Street. It was vacation time and my secretary had gone on hers, so I handed Mrs. Denovo a notebook and gave her some letters. And she was so good I kept her."

"Had she been sent by an agency?"

"No. I asked who had sent her, and she said nobody, she had heard someone say I needed a stenographer."

"But you checked on her references."

"I never asked her for any. Three days was enough to see how good she was, not only as a stenographer, and I didn't bother. After a week I didn't give a damn where she had worked before or how she happened to walk in that morning. It didn't matter."

I closed the notebook and stuck it in my pocket. "But that makes it a blank. First you tell me to forget everybody connected with her work here, there's not a chance it was one of them, and now are you saying you know nothing about her before the second of July, nineteen forty-five? What she had done or where she had been?"

"Yes, I am."

"After being closely associated with her for twenty-two years? I don't believe it."

He nodded. "You're not the first detective that can't believe it. Two of them from the police, at different times, couldn't either. But it's—"

"Were they here recently?"

"No, that was back in May, just after her death. But it's true. She never spoke of her family or background—anything you could call personal, and she wasn't a woman you would . . . Well, she kept her distance. I'll give you an example. Once a woman—an important woman, important to us; she represented one of our clients—she was saying something about her sister, and she asked Mrs. Denovo if she had a sister, and she just ignored it. Not even a yes or no. I'm pretty quick at getting on to people, and within a month after I met her, less than that, I knew she had lines I wasn't to cross. And I never did. If you want to ask some of the others here go ahead, but you'll be wasting your time. Do you want to try?"

Ordinarily I would have said yes, and perhaps I should have, but I was only partly there. I had come only because Wolfe had said to. Where I wanted to be was with Avery Ballou. So I said I didn't want to interfere with their lunch hours but I might be back later, tomorrow if not today, and thanked him on behalf of Miss Denovo. He said if I come tomorrow he would have the copies of the photographs by four o'clock, and I thanked him again.

As I went down the hall to the elevator I decided to head for Al's diner and treat myself to bacon and eggs and home-fried potatoes. Eggs are never fried in Wolfe's and Fritz's kitchen, and neither are potatoes, but that wasn't the main point. The idea of sitting through lunch with Wolfe and discussing something like the future of computers or the effect of organized sport on American culture, when we should be discussing how to handle Avery Ballou, didn't appeal to me.

But knowing that Wolfe had done his reflecting and was as keen to go at Ballou as I was, I reflected as I sipped coffee and decided it would do him good to be stalled off a little, say half an hour, to even up for my being stalled by his sappy rule about table talk. So I

watched the time. I left the diner at two on the dot
walked the three blocks to the old brownstone, and entered the office at 2:05, got the retainer from the safe
went across the hall to the dining-room door, and said
"You said to deposit this at an early opportunity and
this is it. I'll be back in half an hour."

"No." He put his coffee cup down. "That can wait. We
have a decision to make."

"Sorry," I said, "I like to obey orders," and went.

I admit I didn't loiter walking to Lexington Avenue
and back, but even so I was gone thirty-six minutes. The
television was on and he was standing in the middle of
the room glaring at it. Presumably he had been so riled
that he had picked on the one thing there that would rile
him more. As I put the bankbook in the safe he turned
the television off and went to his desk, and as I went to
mine he demanded, "What the devil has someone done?"

Not "What have you done?"

I crossed my legs. "My lunch was greasy and I ate too
fast. I wanted to get that twenty grand in the bank before
it closed. I hurried back because I knew you wanted to
tell me how to approach Ballou. But first, of course, you
want a full report on Raymond Thorne."

"I do not. Unless you got something that makes it unnecessary to see Mr. Ballou."

"I didn't. Except for two photographs of Elinor Denovo
I drew a blank. A complete blank. Have you phoned to
find out if he's there?"

"No. You will."

"Sure. A corporation president might be anywhere in
August. If I get him do I ask to see him today? I suppose
you've decided how I play it."

"Not you." He cleared his throat. "Archie. You have
many aptitudes, some of them extraordinary, but it will
be delicate and may be thorny. Besides, it was I who
dealt with him before. You were present, but I did it. I
must be sure of the facts. You said on the telephone that
the checks cashed by Mrs. Denovo were drawn by the
Seaboard Bank and Trust Company, payable to bearer
How sure is that?"

"The only way to make it any surer would be to look
at them. It came straight from the top man at the Eighty-

sixth Street branch of the Continental, where she cashed a hundred of them. His name's Atwood."

"And Mr. Ballou is now a director of the Seaboard Bank and Trust Company?"

"He is unless he quit or has been bounced very recently. It was this year's edition of Rand McNally's *International Bank Directory*."

"How difficult would it be to learn about the checks without Mr. Ballou's help?"

"Close to impossible. The Seaboard is a two-billion-dollar outfit. Their main office probably draws thousands of checks in a year, maybe tens of thousands, drawn by God knows how many clerks. And of course they have automation. I don't see how we could even start. I suppose we could have Sue Corbett, or Miss Denovo herself, get to some assistant vice-president and seduce him, and if it didn't work try another one, and in a year or so—"

"Get Mr. Ballou."

"You'll talk?"

"No. It will be more exigent from you. Tell him that if it will suit his convenience I would like to see him, here, at six o'clock."

I wheeled my chair and reached for the book, got the number of the Federal Holding Corporation, and dialed. Once before, when I had tried for Ballou on the phone, it had taken three people to get me through, and this time it was the same—first the switchboard female, then another female who made me spell my name twice, and then a man. They were all so reserved that I didn't even know if he was there until his voice came.

"Goodwin? *Archie* Goodwin?"

"Right." Knowing the voice, I went on. "I'm glad I got you. I'm calling for Mr. Wolfe. If it will suit your convenience he would like to see you, here at his office, at six o'clock, or as soon after that as you can make it."

Silence; then: "Today?"

"Yes. It's a little urgent."

A longer silence, and of course I knew why. He couldn't ask what was up. He couldn't ask anything on a phone that someone else might be on. But he did. He asked, "Will it take long?"

"Probably not. Half an hour ought to do it."

A shorter silence; then: "I'll be there at six." He hung up.

I cradled it, turned to Wolfe, who had listened in, and said, "He'll be expecting a holy mess," and Wolfe said he should be relieved to find there wasn't one. He looked at the clock, saw that he had an hour before leaving for the plant rooms, and told me to take my notebook. There was still unanswered mail from last week.

At 5:30, having finished the dozen or so letters he had given me, I went up to my room to change my shirt, because the walk to the bank and back with the temperature twenty degrees above what it was in that air-conditioned house had worked up a sweat, but I was down again in twenty minutes, so I was there when Wolfe came down. As he reached his desk the doorbell rang.

I believe I mentioned somewhere in my report of the death of a doxy that Avery Ballou's face was seamy but had no sag. Now, I saw as I opened the door and let him in, it did have a sag. But he was trying to look grim and ready for anything, and that didn't go very well with the sag. He didn't walk, he strode, down the hall and on in. As he sat in the red leather chair, not settled back, after acknowledging Wolfe's greeting with a nod that wasn't cordial at all, he rubbed his brow with a palm. I had seen him do that before, more than once, when he *had* been in a mess.

His hand dropped to grip the chair arm. "I'm not accust—" he began, but it came out hoarse and he stopped. He started over. "I'm not in the habit of getting a peremptory summons from a—from anybody."

Wolfe nodded. "I suppose not. But I needed to see you. You may remember that I never leave my house on business errands, but there was also the consideration that you would probably prefer not to have Mr. Goodwin or me call at your office. First I'll—"

"Why do you need to see me?"

"I'll tell you in a moment. First I'll relieve your mind. My need has no connection with what happened eighteen months ago, none whatever. No connection with you or your affairs. I am having—"

"Then goddam it, why did—"

"If you please. I am having a rare experience, almost without precedent. I am embarrassed. I need to say something and I am unsure about how to say it. I must ask your help on a problem, and how do I do it without risking misunderstanding?"

"I don't know. I never saw you at a loss for words. Is that straight? It has nothing to do with me?"

"Yes. It's *my* problem. And Mr. Goodwin's."

Ballou took a deep breath, settled back in the chair, turned to me, and said, "I could use a drink."

"Gin on the rocks with lemon peel?" I asked. "There's fresh mint if you want it."

"You remember? I'll be damned. No mint."

I didn't move; I didn't intend to miss the next five minutes. Wolfe, seeing I wasn't going, pushed a button, and when Fritz came gave him a triple order: gin for the guest, beer for him, and milk for me.

He squinted at Ballou. "It's difficult. I can't pretend that you are under any obligation to me. You paid me a substantial sum for the ticklish and knotty job I did for you. You did say that you had to be rescued from that predicament no matter what it cost, but that was merely the desperate squawk of a man under intolerable pressure. The account was settled. You owe me nothing. But the fact remains that Mr. Goodwin and I remain in possession of a secret which you still wish to protect at any cost, and we could support our knowledge with evidence. Then no matter what I say, how I put it, how can I ask you to help me on a problem without risking an indictment for extortion? For blackmail? Not by a jury; by you."

He compressed his lips and shook his head. "Confound it. Words won't do it. No words will erase or suspend your awareness that I could divulge that secret. There are no conceivable circumstances in which Mr. Goodwin or I *would* divulge it, but you know we could, and I can't open your skull and select those cells and remove them."

He shook his head some more. "I'll try another tack. I need your help. I presume to request it solely on the supposition that you may be willing to supply it not to meet any obligation, but to show your continued appreciation for the service I rendered you. If your appreciation has withered or vanished, I make no request."

"It hasn't." The sag was gone, and Ballou had even smiled a couple of times. "It's too bad you didn't know how to say it. I'm glad you're not going to open my skull, I appreciate that, too. What's your problem?"

That had to wait because Fritz came with the drinks. He served Wolfe's beer first, the bottle unopened because that's a rule, and Wolfe got his opener from the drawer, a gold one Marko Vukcic had given him that didn't work very well. By the time Fritz had served my milk and had gone, Ballou had downed a good half of his gin, but the bottle and ice were there on the stand.

Wolfe licked foam from his lips and eyed Ballou. "Well," he said, "I did my best. Making the request is much simpler. According to Mr. Goodwin, you are a director of the Seaboard Bank and Trust Company."

He nodded. "I'm on the board. I'm on several boards. Eight, I think."

"Indeed. I don't know much about boards, but I assume a director is on speaking terms with the people who do the work. Now the problem. Twenty-two years ago, in June nineteen forty-five, someone got a bank check from the Seaboard Bank and Trust Company for one thousand dollars, payable to bearer. Call him X. The next month, July, he got another bank check for the same amount, and the next, and the next. That continued through month after month and year after year—two hundred and sixty-four checks in twenty-two years. The last one was in May of this year; there have been none since and there will be none. I need to know who X is. I must ask him something. That's my problem."

Ballou took a sip of gin. "What's the rest of it?"

"There isn't any 'rest.' That's it."

"My God. All this performance, getting me here and all your jabber, for something as simple as that?"

"I didn't know it would be simple."

"Well, it is. It would be even simpler if the checks were to a specific payee instead of bearer, but it's still simple, since it was the same amount every month for twenty-two years. All it will take is some digging by a clerk. Goodwin could have asked me on the phone. I'll call him tomorrow, or someone at Seaboard will." He took a sip. "You gave me a good scare and I certainly don't appreciate that, but now that I'm here I might as well say that I still fully appreciate what you did for me when I needed help a hell of a lot more than you do now." He emptied the glass and put it down. "How's the detective business?" He turned to me. "I'm surprised at you, Goodwin. He may not have known how simple it was, since he doesn't get out and around, but you should have. I'll have someone give you a ring tomorrow."

He got up, offered Wolfe a shake, and came to give me one too. I escorted him to the front and out, and when I returned to the office told Wolfe, "Not the one he had last year, a new one. It isn't true that everyone keeps his Rolls Royce forever."

You may be agreeing with Ballou, that all that performance, scaring him into coming and Wolfe's long and eloquent speech, which I wouldn't call jabber, was unnecessary, but you shouldn't. He didn't know that X was almost certainly a father who didn't want to be spotted and might possibly be a murderer, but you do. You may also be thankful that you have seen and heard the last of Ballou except for a brief phone call that would be just routine, but if so you have an unwelcome surprise coming. I got a surprise too, at a quarter past six the next afternoon, Tuesday, when the doorbell rang and I went to the hall and saw Ballou on the stoop.

I had guessed earlier that it hadn't been quite so simple, when no phone call came. Expecting it, I had stayed in all day, except for a quick trip to the mailbox on the corner, but at four o'clock, having called Raymond Thorne and learned that the copies of the photographs were ready, I told Wolfe I was flipping the switch for the plant rooms for incoming calls and went for a walk. It was even hotter outdoors than the day before and I was glad to get back to the air-conditioned brownstone. The copies were fine, just as good as the originals. At 6:15 Wolfe, at his desk, was looking them over when the doorbell rang and I went. When I told him it was Ballou he grunted, and when I ushered him in the photographs were not in sight.

Ballou didn't offer a hand. He got settled in the red leather chair, apparently expecting to be there a while. His face had no sag. He aimed his eyes at Wolfe and said, "I would give something to know how much you knew yesterday."

Wolfe adjusted his bulk. It looked as if it was going to take another performance. "You don't mean that," he said. "It's much too broad. I knew innumerable things that wouldn't interest you. If you confine it to what I knew about the identity of X, the answer is nothing. I not only had no knowledge, I had no basis for a conjecture. I was completely—"

"You talk too much. You knew why you wanted to know. You knew why it was important enough to get me here. You can tell me that now, and you will."

Wolfe's head retreated to the chair's high back and his eyes closed. Often, when some visitor gives him a tough one, he looks at me, but that wouldn't help with that one. It was too simple. Stalling wouldn't help. Maneuvering might do it, just possibly, but with that buck probably not. And after all, telling him wouldn't hurt either the job or the client. I figured it like that in about ten seconds, and so did he. He opened his eyes, moved his head, and said, "I would have told you that yesterday if you had asked. A young woman has engaged me to learn who her father was. Or is. I have reason to suppose that it would be relevant to know who had those checks drawn. To tell you my client's name would violate a confidence, and I—"

He stopped because he had lost his audience. Ballou's head was back and he was laughing good and loud. Wolfe looked at me and I put my palms and my brows up. Ballou finished his laugh, gave both of us a broad smile, and said, "Wonderful. By God, this is good. He shelled out for twenty-two years? I'll be damned."

"Evidently you know him."

"I certainly do. Does it help to know that the checks were endorsed by Elinor Denovo?"

"It doesn't hurt. That isn't the name of my client, but it's pertinent. Since you know him . . . Mr. Ballou. There should be no misunderstanding. If you name him, and I hope you will, I can't engage to regard it as a confidence. I'll use it as required in the interest of my client."

"I would expect you to." Ballou was enjoying himself. The laugh was still in his eyes. "A couple of hours ago I didn't think I was going to name him; I was going to phone you that the information you wanted wasn't available, but I decided to come and find out why you wanted it. Now that you've told me I *will* name him. Provided—you're not stringing me? It's just that, a woman wants to know who her father was? Is."

"Yes. It's just that. The name of the endorser, Elinor Denovo, makes it certain that the name you know is the one I need."

"I'll be damned. Wonderful. How old is the woman?"

"Twenty-two. The first check came two weeks after she was born."

"Let's see . . . twenty-two from seventy-six; he was fifty-four. I didn't know him then as well as I do now. His name is Jarrett, Cyrus M. Jarrett. Nothing about this is confidential, what I'm telling you now, it's known by everybody in banking circles. Twenty-two years ago he was the president of Seaboard. In nineteen fifty-three—he was sixty-two then—he became Chairman of the Board. Some of us wanted him out of management entirely, but he had a big block of stock and that wasn't all he had. He's a very wealthy man. At sixty-five he should have retired, that's usual, but he wouldn't. But by then a majority of us—of the board—wanted him out, and we finally managed it. That was in nineteen fifty-nine, eight years ago. He's still on the board, but he seldom comes to meetings."

He paused to enjoy a smile, not for us, it was private. He went on. "All that is known to everybody, of course. I'm telling you because you might wonder why I was willing to name him. I never liked him and I don't like him now. A lot of people don't. As for being confidential, I don't give a damn if it becomes known that I helped you find him. I doubt if you'll be able to make him lose any sleep, nobody ever has, but I wish you luck. If you have any questions I'll be glad—"

He looked at his watch. "No, I won't." He stood up. "I was late yesterday, and I'll be late again now if the traffic's bad." He headed for the door, turned to say, "Come to my office, Goodwin, if you have questions," and moved so fast that I would have had to trot to open the door for him, so I didn't go.

As the sound came of the front door closing, Wolfe looked at the clock. Dinner in thirty-five minutes. He looked at me. "Do you like it?"

"Well." I pinched my nose. "I'm not going to jump up and down and yell three cheers for us. So he's old and tough. If he was fifty-four in nineteen forty-five he's seventy-six now. I've read a few things about him, there was a piece about him in *Fortune* once and I read it, but that doesn't give me an in."

"You have Miss Denovo's telephone number?"

"Certainly."

"Get her. I'll talk."

I consulted my pocket notebook to check the number, swung the phone around and dialed, and while I waited decided to say Archie Goodwin, not just Archie. I didn't care to give Wolfe a peg for another of his rusty comments about what he called my aptitude for establishing personal relations with young women. When the hello came, her voice, I said, "Amy Denovo?"

"Yes. Archie?"

That changed the script. "Right. I'm calling from the office. Mr. Wolfe wants to talk."

He had his phone. I kept mine. "This is Nero Wolfe, Miss Denovo. I need to ask a question. Has your telephone an extension?"

"No."

"I'll be circumspect anyway. I don't like the telephone and I don't trust it. Don't ask indiscreet questions. We have discovered the source of the checks. The informa—"

"You have? Already?"

"It isn't necessary to interrupt. I'll tell you all that is tellable on this machine. The information about the source is reliable—in fact, certain. We know who had the checks drawn. He is alive, seventy-six years old, wealthy, retired, of what is called the upper class. He lives in New York—no, I don't know that, but I do know he's reachable. So I have a question. You know what you hired me to do. The source of the checks is established, but not that he is himself the person you want found. That is merely a reasonable surmise. Do you want me to—"

"I want to know his name!"

"You will. If you'll come this evening, at nine o'clock or

after, we'll tell you. What I ask now: Do you want me to proceed with the inquiry or do you want to deal with him yourself? I would like to know that before dinner."

"I want you to do it, of course. I'll come now. I—may I come now?"

"No. In the middle of a meal? We'll expect you later."

He hung up, got the photographs from the drawer, frowned at them, and dropped them on the desk. I swung my phone back and asked, "Shall I ring Cyrus M. Jarrett and tell him you want him here at eleven tomorrow morning if it will suit his convenience?"

"Yes," he hissed. He never hisses. He got up and went to the kitchen.

6

At half past three Wednesday afternoon I sat in an all-weather chair under a maple tree on top of a cliff in Dutchess County. To my right was a scenic view of three or four miles of the Hudson River. About a hundred yards to my left was an ivy-covered end of a mansion or palace or castle which must have had between thirty and fifty rooms, depending on their size. In every direction there were bushes, trees, flowers, things like a statue of a deer eating out of a girl's hand, and grass. Lily Rowan's glade had never seen grass like that. Eight feet in front of me, on a chair like mine but with an attached footrest, was a lean, lengthy man with a long bony face, an ample crop of white hair, and a pair of gray-blue eyes so cold that, taking them straight, you got no impression at all. At half past three I was saying to him, "That was just a dodge. I have no silver abacus. In fact, I have never seen one."

Having spent the morning at the public library and the *Gazette* morgue, I knew enough about Cyrus M. Jarrett to fill a dozen pages, but you don't care or need to know that it was his left leg he broke when he fell off a horse in 1958. Here are a few items. His grandfather had paid for the palace; Cyrus M. had been born in it. He had had one wife, who had died in 1943, one daughter, now living in Rome with her husband, who was a count, and one son, named Eugene E., forty-three years old, one of the nine vice-presidents of the Seaboard Bank and Trust Company I had seen listed in the *International Bank Directory*. Cyrus M. was a member of nine boards of directors, topping Ballou by one. During the Second World War he had been a member of the Production Allotment Board. And so forth and so on.

The one essential item for me was that he used six of the rooms in the palace to house one of the three finest known collections of Colonial handiwork; that was the one I had used to get to him. At the library, after spotting that in the *Fortune* piece, I had consulted the library files and got a book, and in half an hour I had realized it would take a month to learn enough to put up a front for five minutes, so I created a piece of handiwork then and there, in my mind, went to a phone booth, and dialed area code 914 and a number.

The male voice that answered had to know precisely what I wanted to see Mr. Jarrett about, and I told him: a silver abacus made by Paul Revere that was in my possession. He told me to hold the wire, and in five minutes came back on and said that Mr. Jarrett said that Paul Revere never made a silver abacus. I said the hell he didn't, tell him I've got it right here in my hand. It worked. After another wait he came back again and said Mr. Jarrett would see me and the abacus at three o'clock.

When I arrived, on the hour, I was shown the chairs under the maple tree and told that Mr. Jarrett would be with me shortly. "Shortly" ran into twenty-two minutes, one for each year of Amy's life, which I would have regarded as a good sign if I believed in signs. As he approached I noted that he looked his seventy-six, but he walked more like fifty-six. Then he got closer and sat and I saw the eyes, and they looked like a thousand and seventy-six. He got his feet up before he said, "Where is it?"

"That was just a dodge," I said. "I have no silver abacus. In fact, I have never seen one."

He turned his head and sang out, "Oscar!"

"But," I said, "I have something for you. A message from your daughter."

"My daughter? You're a liar."

"Not Catherine. Amy. Amy Denovo." I glanced at the man who had left the house and was coming. "It's very—personal."

"You're not only a liar, you're an idiot."

"I'll be glad to discuss that, but I'd rather do it private-ly."

The man arrived. He stopped two steps from Jarrett's chair and stood. "You called, sir?"

Jarrett, not looking at him, said, "I thought I wanted something, but I don't. Leave."

The man turned and went. I said, "I didn't know that was still being done. What have you got on him?"

He said, "Who are you?"

"I gave my name on the phone, Archie Goodwin. I work for a private detective named Nero Wolfe. The message from Amy is that now, since her mother is dead, she would like to know something about her father."

"I could have you kicked out," he said, "but I prefer to let you commit yourself so I can have the police come and get you. I called you an idiot because anybody with any sense would know how I would treat a blackmailer and you must be one. Go ahead, commit yourself."

"I already have." I was leaning back, comfortable. "It *would* be a spot for a little fancy blackmailing, but Amy has paid Mr. Wolfe a good big retainer and we're committed to her. Of course it's your money, or it was. It came out of what you sent her mother, for her."

"Go ahead."

"Look, Mr. Jarrett." I was meeting the frozen eyes and it wasn't easy to talk to them. "We didn't have to handle it like this. We could have let you wait and started digging away back for details. But that would have taken time and money, and all Amy wanted was to find you. I can't give you a written guarantee, but I doubt very much if she wants to start any fuss, try to make you acknowledge her, or anything like that. She might possibly want some money, but what the hell, you've got ten times more than you need. And don't get the idea that I'm just out fishing. We know all about the checks. We know they came from you, two hundred and sixty-four of them; that's on the record. We know they were endorsed by Elinor Denovo." I flipped a hand. "Now you talk a while."

"Go ahead, go ahead. What do *you* want? What does this Nero Wolfe want?"

"Mr. Wolfe wants nothing. As for me, what would

please me most would be something like this: you have Oscar call the cops and tell them to come and get me. When they come you tell them I tried to blackmail you, and I clam up, and they take me somewhere for questioning—the sheriff's office or a state barracks. It will be a pipe to handle it so they hold me, and then look out for the dust. For a start, our lawyer and a newspaperman I know—the *Gazette*. Today's Wednesday. By Friday ten million people will be sympathizing with you—all this trouble after twenty-two years. Of course we won't give them Amy's name, but that won't matter, it's your name that's newsworthy. Do you want me to call Oscar, or would you rather?"

The goddam eyes hadn't even blinked, I swear they hadn't, but the bony jaw had flicked once or twice. I was beginning to understand why a lot of people didn't like him. People want people to react. He did finally say something. He said, "Those checks are in the files of the Seaboard Bank and Trust Company. Who told you about them?"

I shook my head. Ballou had said he didn't give a damn if it became known that he had helped us find him, but I was giving this character nothing. "That's beside the point," I said. "The checks, endorsed by Elinor Denovo, are the point. I have a suggestion. You and I aren't hitting it off very well. I'll bring Amy tomorrow, and that may work better. She's okay. She's a very nice girl. As you probably know, she graduated from Smith, she has good looks and good manners, she wouldn't—"

I stopped because he was moving. He took his time getting his feet around and on the grass, turning on his rump, and getting upright. The eyes came down at me. "I know nothing," he said, "of any Amy, and nothing of any Elinor Denovo. If there is an Elinor Denovo and she endorsed checks that had been charged to my account, I don't know how they came into her hands and I am not concerned. If you publish any of this rubbish I'll get your hide." He turned and headed for the house.

It was a nice place to sit, with the view of the river and all the flowers and leaves, and I sat. Soon after Jarrett had entered the house Oscar came out and stationed himself in the shade of a tree with long narrow

leaves. I called to him, "What kind of a tree is that?" but
got no answer. It would have been interesting to stay put
for an hour or so and see how long he would stand there
with nothing to do, but I was thirsty and doubted if he
would leave his post to bring me a drink, so I moved.
The direct route to where the Heron was parked took me
right past him, but I pretended he wasn't there.

The winding blacktop driveway was a good quarter of
a mile. At its end, with its twenty-foot stone pillars, I
turned left, and in about a mile right, and in twenty minutes, counting a stop for a root beer, I was at the entrance
to the Taconic State Parkway, southbound. A sign said:
NEW YORK 88 MILES. I never try to do any deep thinking
while I'm driving; the thinking gets you nowhere and the
driving might get you where you would rather not be;
and anyway there was nothing much to think about, since
I knew what would come next. Wolfe and I had agreed on
that, without argument, in case I got a brushoff from Jarrett, after Amy left Tuesday evening.

I had promised I would let her know what happened,
so I left the Henry Hudson Parkway at Ninety-sixth
Street and took the Eighty-fifth Street transverse through
Central Park. Trying to find a legal space at the curb
would be like trying to find room for another kernel on
an ear of corn, and I drove to the garage on Second Avenue where Elinor Denovo had kept her car. Don't ask me
how or why, but I have always had a feeling that it helps
to see places that are in any way connected with a job,
even if they tell you nothing. Walking to Amy's address
I took the route Elinor had taken the last time she had
walked, and I saw that it would have been no trick at all,
at that time of night, for someone who knew she had
her car out, to park near the corner on Second Avenue,
see her arrive in her car, and see her leave the garage and
turn into Eighty-third Street. By then of course he would
have had the engine started and would be ready to go.

I didn't give Amy a verbatim report. We rarely do to
clients; they'll always ask why you didn't tell him this or
that, or what you said that for, or you should have
realized he was lying. Also I didn't tell her what was next
on the program. That's even worse; they'll object for some
cockeyed reason or they'll have something better to sug-

gest. When I had given her the facts that mattered, her big question was whether I thought Jarrett was her father, and of course I passed. I told her that while it was still the best guess that he was, I wouldn't personally risk a buck either way. I tried to get out of her exactly what she intended to do when we finally got it pinned down, but when I left I still didn't know and I doubted if she did. Apparently that was open and she wouldn't know the answer herself until she knew for sure who her father was.

It was only ten minutes to dinnertime when I got home, so the verbatim report had to wait until we had taken on the curried beef roll, celery and cantaloupe salad, and blueberry grunt, and had gone to the office for coffee. When I had finished, including my stopover at Amy's, his first question was typical. He emptied the coffee pot into his cup, took a sip, and said, "I think it's quite possible that Paul Revere did make a silver abacus. What gave you the notion?"

I tapped my skull with knuckles. "You said once that the more you put in a brain the more it will hold. What about the things that come out that were never put in? That's why I can't answer your question."

"They had been put in. 'Paul Revere' was there and 'silver' was there and 'abacus' was there. The question you can't answer is what joined them when for the first and only time in your life their juncture would meet a need, and I concede that it's unanswerable. I withdraw it." He drank coffee. "Will you telephone Mr. Ballou in the morning or see him?"

"See him. I can't show him a photograph on the phone."

"Will Mr. Jarrett do anything, and if he does, what?"

"To the first, I doubt it. To the second, I couldn't guess. Of course you realize that if that hit-and-run was murder, not just homicide, it's possible that the client is now a mark. If you ask me if I think it's conceivable that that rich, retired, respectable upper-class citizen stole a car and ran it over a hard-working respectable middle-class woman, the answer is yes. That tough old fish-eyed buzzard? Yes."

He nodded. "It's remote, but . . . did you warn her?"

"No. It's more than remote, it's up in the moon, which they haven't reached yet. From what I said and didn't say, he knows that all we've got is the checks. So if Elinor knew or threatened something that made it necessary to cross her out, he has no reason to suspect that she passed it on to Amy. I can ring her and tell her to be ready to jump when she crosses streets, but she might get a wrong impression. She might think she's more on my mind than the job is."

"Very well." His shoulders went up an eighth of an inch and down again. I have mentioned his screwy notion about young women and me. He removed the paperweight, a chunk of jade that a woman, not young, had used years ago to conk her husband, from some items on his desk. "If your evening is free, I have three or four letters."

I said half of the evening was already gone and got my notebook.

Thursday morning I made a mistake I often make, crowding my luck. That's fine when it works, but too often it doesn't. Instead of ringing Avery Ballou for an appointment I just went, arriving a little after ten, and as a result I spent two hours in a reception room on the thirty-fourth floor of a forty-story financial castle on Wall Street. Mr. Ballou was in conference. That means anything from scouting around for indigestion pills to presiding at a gathering to decide something that will affect the future of thousands of people, but whatever it meant that morning, it was affecting my present. There was plenty for the eye in the marble-walled room, people coming and going and sitting around waiting and worrying, but I was too sore at my luck to get any fun out of it. It was five minutes past noon when a handsome junior financier came and took me inside and led me along a hall and around a corner to Ballou's room.

It had six windows, five upholstered leather chairs, two other doors, and I suppose other things to fit, but that was all my glance caught as I crossed to Ballou. There was a king-size desk near the far end, but he was standing at a window. If he was sorry he had kept me waiting so long he didn't mention it.

"What a morning," he said. "I can give you five minutes, Goodwin."

"That might do it," I said. I took something from a pocket. "You told us that the checks were endorsed by

Elinor Denovo. Here are two photographs of her, taken twenty years ago." I handed them to him. "Can you place her?"

He gave them a good look, taking half of one of the five minutes, then shook his head. "No, I can't. You say it's Elinor Denovo?"

"Right. That's certain."

"And she endorsed the checks. And you're expecting to connect her with Jarrett. Twenty years ago, that was nineteen forty-seven. I hadn't known him long then, and I never have known him as a—socially. Practically all my contacts with him have been business." He handed me the photographs. "Of course you think it's important to connect her."

"It's essential."

He went to the king-size desk, sat, pushed a button, and said, "Get Mr. McCray at Seaboard." I'm glad we don't have an intercom at the old brownstone. It would annoy me to be up in my room ready for a shower and just as I reached to turn it on hear Wolfe's voice, "Where's that letter from Mr. Hewitt?"

Ballou didn't have to wait long. There was a buzz and he took a phone. "Ballou. . . . Good morning, Bert. A man named Archie Goodwin is here. . . . That's right, I told you yesterday, for Nero Wolfe. . . . He has asked me a question I can't answer, but you probably could. Can I send him over? It wouldn't take long. . . . Yes, of course. . . . No, he's presentable, jacket, tie—hell, he's neater than I am. . . . Good. I knew you would."

He hung up and turned to me. "You'll have lunch at the Bankers Club with Bertram McCray." He spelled the McCray. "One-twenty Broadway. He'll be there in ten minutes. Check in as McCray's guest. He's a vice-president at Seaboard. Twenty years ago he was Jarrett's secretary and protégé; he was often at his home. He has a grudge because Jarrett didn't move up around nineteen fifty and make him president—of course that was absurd —and he switched to our side in fifty-three. He got that information for me yesterday about the checks. He said he'd like to meet Nero Wolfe, so ask him anything you want to. Have you got that?"

I said yes and he pushed a button and said, "Ready for that man from Boston."

So at one o'clock I was seated at a table by a wall in a room with about a hundred other tables. With an average of three men to a table, I supposed around twenty billion dollars was represented, either in person or by proxy. I was certainly glad I had a necktie on. My host, facing me, had ears that were a little too big and a nose that was a little too small, and a slight pinch at the corner of his right eye. He was either very polite or he had no initiative; when I had chosen sole *Véronique* and salad and lemon ice he had taken the same. We were both polite, though; we talked about the heat wave and air pollution and the summer crop of riots until we had finished the sole and salad, but as we waited for the ices and coffee he said he only took an hour for lunch and Ballou had told him I wanted to ask him something. I said Ballou had told me that he had known Cyrus M. Jarrett for many years and might be able to identify a woman Nero Wolfe wanted to know about, and produced the photographs and handed them to him. He looked at the top one, the three-quarters face, widened his eyes at me, looked at the profile, then again at the other one, and again at me.

"Why," he said, "it's Lottie Vaughn."

I tried not to bat an eye. "Good," I said. "At least we have her name. Who is Lottie Vaughn?" But I realized I was being silly; I had told Ballou. So I went on, "The name we have is Elinor Denovo. Those pictures are of her, taken twenty years ago."

"I don't see . . ." He was frowning. "I don't get it." He looked at the photographs. "This is Carlotta Vaughn, I'm absolutely certain. What do you mean, it's Elinor Denovo?"

"Those are the only pictures we have of her," I said, "and we need them." I put out a hand. As he hesitated the waiter came with the ices and coffee, and I let him go on hesitating until we were served and the waiter had gone, then reached again and he handed them over. "It's a long story," I said, "and most of it is confidential information from our client. From what Mr. Ballou told me I don't think you would pass anything on to Jarrett.

I know you wouldn't, but you're a banker and you know it's always better to be too careful than not careful enough. You also know that Mr. Wolfe is hoping and expecting to get Jarrett out on a limb. So I'll appreciate it if you'll tell me about Carlotta Vaughn. Did Jarrett know her?"

He nodded. "That's where I met her. At his home."

"Was she a guest?"

"No. She was Mrs. Jarrett's secretary when I met her. When Mrs. Jarrett died he kept her. I was his secretary then, dividing my time between his home—his homes— and the office, and you might say she was my assistant. She was very intelligent and competent."

The ices didn't get eaten and not much of the coffee was drunk, and McCray's hour for lunch got stretched. That was one of the times that my memory, which I'll match with anybody, came in handy, because I didn't want to take out my notebook. I doubted if my host would approve there with all those billions around. I submit these facts about Carlotta Vaughn, of course all of them according to Bertram McCray.

He had first seen her at the Jarrett town house in New York, when she had started as Mrs. Jarrett's secretary, in May 1942. She had continued at that job until November 1943, when Mrs. Jarrett had died of cancer, and then had stayed to work for Jarrett. At that time McCray had been spending about two-thirds of his time at the bank and one-third at the house, either in town or in the country, and she was extremely useful. She almost never did anything at the bank, only two or three times in four or five months.

As for her background, he knew she had come from Wisconsin, some small town near Milwaukee, and that was all. He didn't know how long she had been in New York, or where she had gone to school, or how she had got the job with Mrs. Jarrett.

So much for her entrance. Where he flunked worst was on her exit. Since starting with Mrs. Jarrett she had lived there, town and country; and in the early spring of 1944, he thought late in March, she suddenly wasn't there, but she might still have been doing something for Jarrett because she came to the house three or four times in the

next six or seven months. The last time he saw her was in
late September or early October 1944, when she spent
part of an evening with Jarrett in the library.

Exit. Curtain.

He wasn't much more helpful on relationships. He had
liked her and admired her, and he thought she had liked
him, but he had been married just the year before, at the
age of thirty, and his first son had just been born, so his
intimate concerns were elsewhere. He remembered vague-
ly that he had got the idea that something might be
developing between her and Jarrett's son Eugene, who
was twenty years old in 1944, but he recalled no specific
incidents. On her relations with Jarrett himself, he had an
internal tussle that was so apparent that I had one too, to
keep from grinning. Of course he knew from Ballou what
we expected to get on Jarrett, and he would have loved
to help by supplying some good salty evidence, but he had
been born either too honest or too shy on invention. He
rang the changes on what was obvious, that Jarrett and
Carlotta were alone together a lot, but when he tried to
remember that he had seen things that had made him
suspect that Carlotta's services weren't exclusively secre-
tarial, he couldn't make it.

That's what my memory took home for me. I accom-
panied him on the short walk back to his job, for a look
at the main office of the Seaboard Bank and Trust Company from the outside, thanked him for the lunch, and
spent ten minutes on the toughest job in New York, finding a vacant hack. I finally beat a guy with a limp to
one. When it rolled to a stop in front of the old brownstone at twenty minutes to three, I had arranged in my
mind a draft all ready for the typewriter. As follows:

CARLOTTA VAUGHN RÉSUMÉ
from Bertram McCray, August 24, 1967

Up to May 1942
　　Not known, but according to her via McCray, some-
　　where in Wisconsin for most of it.
May 1942, to November 1943
　　Mrs. Jarrett's secretary. Lived there.

November 1943, to March 1944

Jarrett's home secretary. Lived there.

March 1944, to October 1944, which includes the month Amy was conceived.

Living elsewhere, presumably in or near New York, since McCray saw her at Jarrett's house three or four times.

October 1944, to July 2, 1945, which includes April 12, 1945, Amy's birthday.

Nothing known.

July 2, 1945

Elinor Denovo walked in on Raymond Thorne.

7

When, at five minutes to six that afternoon, I braked the Heron to a stop at the edge of the gravel in front of the main entrance to the Jarrett mansion, it was dark enough for midnight. Clouds had been making passes as far south as Hawthorne Circle. At Shrub Oak they had closed ranks, and at Millbrook they had cut loose on three fronts: for the ears, noise to scare you; for the eyes, flashes to blind you; and for the skin, water to soak you. It stayed right with me the rest of the way, and having made it to my destination in spite of the big try at stopping me, I turned off the engine and pocketed the key, switched the lights off, reached to the back seat for my raincoat, the spare that is always there, draped it over my head, opened the door, and dashed across the gravel for cover.

My reception was fully down to expectations. It was Oscar who opened the door after I had pushed the button three times. In the circumstances it wasn't only natural, it was compulsory, for any fellow being to say "Quite a storm" or "Are you wet?" or "Nice day for ducks." He barely gave me room enough to enter without brushing him.

I was expected. Often, after I make a report to Wolfe, there is a long discussion, and sometimes an argument which stops just short of me quitting or him firing me, about what comes next, but that time it had been obvious. The discussion had lasted maybe three minutes, then I had pulled the phone around and dialed area code 914 and a number, and got the same male voice I had got the day before. I didn't know if it was Oscar because Oscar in person had said very little in my hearing.

"This is Archie Goodwin," I said. "I was there yester-day. Please tell Mr. Jarrett that I am coming again. I'll be there in about two hours."

"I can't do that, Mr. Goodwin. Mr. Jarrett has given orders that you are not to be admitted. There's a man at the entrance, and he—"

"Yeah. Excuse me for interrupting. I expected that, that's why I'm phoning. Please tell Mr. Jarrett that I want to ask him for some information about Carlotta Vaughn." I repeated the name, distinctly. "Carlotta Vaughn. He'll recognize that name. I'll hold the wire."

"But I assure you, Mr. Goodwin—"

"I assure *you*, sir. He won't thank you for the message, but he'll see me."

A brief silence; then: "Hold the wire."

The wait was longer than the ones the day before. Wolfe, with his receiver in one hand, was adjusting the spray of Miltonia hellemense in the vase on his desk with the other. Finally the voice came.

"Mr. Goodwin?"

"I'm here."

"You say in two hours?"

"More or less. Maybe a little more."

"Very well. You will be admitted."

As I hung up, Wolfe growled, "That creature has been so reduced to chronic subservience that he was deferen-tial even to you. I would like to deal with Mr. Jarrett. I am almost minded to go along."

Just chatter. Before leaving I typed the résumé of the life of Carlotta Vaughn as we knew it, which I had ar-ranged in my mind on the way. You have seen it.

Now, as I put my raincoat on a bench and followed Oscar across a reception hall, along a wide corridor, and around a turn into a narrower hall that took us to an open door at the end, I forgot to observe things because I was too busy looking forward to dealing with Mr. Jarrett. One would have got you ten that this time I would get a reaction. But I did observe the room I entered. It had a fifteen-foot ceiling, a rug twice the size of Lily Rowan's 19-by-34 Kashan, a big desk that was presumably Colonial handiwork, and more books than Wolfe owned, on shelves that reached nearly to the ceiling. Not one of the chairs was occupied. Oscar turned on some lights and said Mr. Jarrett would come shortly, and this time "shortly" was more like it, only a couple of minutes. As he entered by another and narrower door between two tiers of shelves, a dazzle of lightning darted in through the windows, and as he halted and stood after five or six steps, the boom of thunder shook them. Good staging. He focused the frozen eyes on me and said, "What do you want to know about Carlotta Vaughn?"

"It might be better," I said, "for me to tell you first what I already know, or some of it. She was your wife's secretary from May nineteen forty-two until your wife died. She lived here—and at your house in town. You kept her on. She stopped living with you in March nineteen forty-four, and I can't prove that you still kept her, with a different meaning for 'kept,' but there's no law against guessing, and we've only been on this five days." I got something from a pocket. "Here are two photographs of her, taken in nineteen forty-six, but she wasn't Carlotta Vaughn then, she was Elinor Denovo, and her daughter Amy was a year old. Take a look."

I offered them, but he didn't take them. He said, "Who's paying you, Goodwin? Just McCray? He's probably only the errand boy for them—he would be—but you must have their names. If I could prove conspiracy to defame . . . Would you like to pocket ten thousand dollars?"

"Not particularly. That's peanuts. Only last week I took home a box that contained two hundred and forty-four grand—and by the way, it had come from you." I put the photographs back in my pocket. "The checks you sent Elinor Denovo, formerly Carlotta Vaughn—"

"That's enough!" He was reacting. Not the eyes, but the voice. He fired those two words at me as if they were bullets. "This is ridiculous. The brainless idiots. You're expecting to show that I am the father of a girl named Amy, that her mother is the Carlotta Vaughn who once worked for my wife and me and is now known as Elinor Denovo. Is that correct?"

"That's obvious."

"When was this girl Amy born?"

"Two weeks before you sent the first check to Elinor Denovo. April twelfth, nineteen forty-five."

"Then she was conceived in the summer of nineteen forty-four. July, unless the birth was abnormally premature or delayed. I suppose you have a notebook. Get it out."

I wasn't subservient enough yet. I tapped my skull. "I file things here."

"File this. In late May nineteen forty-four I went to England on a mission for the Production Allotment Board to consult with Eisenhower's staff and the British. Seven days after the landing in Normandy I flew to Cairo for more consultations, and then to Italy. On July first I was put to bed with pneumonia in an army hospital in Naples. On July twenty-fourth I was still shaky and I was flown to Marrakech to recuperate. My room in the villa was the one Churchill had once occupied. On August twentieth I flew to London and was there until September sixth, when I returned to Washington. If you had got your notebook when I told you to you'd have those dates." He turned his head and called, "Oscar!"

The door, the big one, opened and Oscar entered and stood with a hand on the knob.

"Brainless idiots," Jarrett said. "Especially McCray; he was born an idiot. If they didn't know how and where I spent that summer they could have found out. Anyone with a spoonful of brains would have. Oscar, this man's going and he isn't coming back." He turned and left by the door he had come in at.

I was in no mood for another waiting match with Oscar. I moved—out by the big door, down the hall and the corridor, and on out. I damn near forgot my raincoat, but the corner of my eye caught it as I was passing, and I got it. I didn't bother to use it crossing the gravel to the car because the downpour had thinned out to a drizzle.

It was just luck that I didn't get a ticket. I usually hold to sixty on the Taconic and the Saw Mill, but I must have hit at least seventy a dozen times and it was probably a personal record for that route. I suppose the idea was that I wanted to get the driving done so I could start thinking, but evidently one thing kept pushing, because at one point on the Saw Mill I braked down, eased off onto the grass, got out my notebook, and jotted down the places and dates Jarrett had rattled off. As I bumped back over the curb to the lane I said out loud, "By God, if I can't even trust my memory I'd better quit."

It was exactly eight o'clock when I mounted the stoop of the old brownstone and used my key, and Wolfe was in the dining room. I stuck my head in at the door and said I'd get a bite in the kitchen, and continued to the rear. Fritz, who always eats his evening meal around nine o'clock, was on his stool at the big center table doing something with artichokes. When I entered he crinkled his eyes at me and said, "Ah. You're back on the feet. Have you eaten?"

"No."

"He was worried about you." He left the stool. "As you know, I never worry about *you*. There's a little mussel bisque—"

"No, thanks. No soup. I want to chew something. Don't tell me he ate a whole duck."

"Oh, no. I knew a man, a Swiss, who ate two ducks." He was at the range, putting on a plate to warm. "Was it a good trip?"

"It was a lousy trip." I was at a cupboard getting out a bottle. "No milk or coffee. I'm going to drink a quart of whisky."

"Not here, Archie. In your room is the place for that. Some *carottes Flamande?*"

I said, "Yes, please," poured a shot of bourbon, sat at my breakfast table, took a swallow, and scowled. Fritz, seeing the scowl, didn't talk.

As I lifted the glass for the third swallow the door swung open and Wolfe was there. He said to Fritz, "I'll have coffee here," and went and mounted the stool at the near side of the center table. Once in the past he had bought a chair big enough for the back of his lap and had it put in the kitchen, but the next day it wasn't there. Fritz had taken it to the basement. As far as I know it has never been mentioned by either of them—not then, and not since.

Another thing that had never been mentioned but was mutually understood was that the rule about talk at meals didn't apply when I was eating alone in the kitchen or office, because it was a snack, not a meal. So when my snack was on my plate and I had chewed and swallowed a man-size morsel of duck Mondor and a forkful of carrots, I told Wolfe, "I appreciate this. You knew I had something on my chest I wanted to unload and you came to have coffee perched on that roost instead of in your chair. I appreciate it."

He made a face. "You're drinking whisky with food."

"It should be hemlock. Who drank hemlock?"

"You're posing. We have discussed that at length more than once. Your chest?"

I was using the knife on the duck—a knife with a wooden handle and a blade dull to the eye but sharp enough to filet a fish. There is plenty of stainless steel up in the plant rooms—the bench frames—but it's taboo in the kitchen or dining room. "This knife would be fine for hara-kiri," I said, "but you'll have to know how it stands so you can carry on. I'll tell you in installments between bites. And swigs of bourbon."

I did so, word for word, a couple of sentences at a time. By the time I got to Jarrett's exit line the carrots were gone and there wasn't much left of my share of the duck but bones, and most of the sauce had been mopped up with pieces of rolls. Wolfe had finished his first cup of coffee and poured the second.

I swallowed the last bite of duck and said, "I don't like the idea of hara-kiri on a full stomach, and anyway I've got about a dime's worth of comments. Do you want to go first?"

"No. You've had two hours to consider it."

"I was driving, not considering. Okay. First, of course, his alibi. Almost certainly it's tight, since he knows it can be checked, but I think Saul or Orrie should be put on it, not only the details but also whether she was with him for any part of it—even granting that he spent the month of July in a hospital with pneumonia. Opinion: it will be a waste of time and money. One will get you fifty that he is not Amy's father. He's too damned sure we're stopped. But I suppose it must be checked."

He nodded. "Orrie. Saul will be needed for chores more difficult."

"He sure will. Now me. It's entirely my fault. Fritz,

I've changed my mind. May I have some coffee? You pour it, please, my hand might shake." I moved my chair around to face Wolfe. "I can't blame it on McCray. Even if he knew all about where Jarrett spent that summer, he didn't know when Amy was born. We hadn't told Ballou, so Ballou hadn't told him. But me? If I had the brains of a half-wit I would have asked McCray where Ballou was during July nineteen forty-four. It's entirely my fault that I drove up there through a cloudburst and invited that ape to push my nose in. Bounce me. Don't pay me for this week. I'll get a job sewing on buttons."

Fritz, who was there pouring coffee, said, "Not if you commit hara-kiri, Archie." He wouldn't have, with Wolfe there, if it had been the dining room or the office, but we were in his kitchen.

"It wasn't wholly futile," Wolfe said. "He gave you confirmation of what had been only a valid assumption, that he knew the date of birth. That's now established. Those places and dates had been arranged in his head before you arrived."

"Uh-huh." I drank coffee and burned my mouth. "Thanks for the bone. That about covers comment. A question, Do I tell the client about Carlotta Vaughn?"

"I think not. Not now. The telephone will do for telling her that we think it highly improbable that Mr. Jarrett sired her. What time is it?" He would have had to pivot his head to ask the kitchen clock.

"Eight thirty-five."

"You'll be late for poker. At Saul's apartment?"

"Yes. It always is."

"If Saul will be free tomorrow morning ask him to come at ten, and call Fred and Orrie. Also at ten. When they come give them everything; they'll need it all and there's nothing we should reserve. You have seen Mr. Jarrett and I haven't. I need your opinion. Elinor Denovo's letter said, 'This money is from your father.' We know it was sent by Mr. Jarrett, the first check two weeks after the birth, but it appears that he is not the father. Well? You have seen him. What impelled him?"

"Yeah, I've seen him." I drank coffee. "And heard him. God only knows. It might be for any one of a thousand reasons, including blackmail, that a man might send a woman a grand every month for twenty-two years, but we decided to take Elinor's letter without salt, and there it is, *this money is from your father.* She couldn't have meant it came direct from Amy's father because it didn't, unless we crack Jarrett's alibi, and we won't. But she knew it came from Jarrett. Even if there was no understanding or arrangement, the checks were Seaboard Bank and Trust Company, and she knew they were from Jarrett. So *this money is from your father* really meant *this money was sent to me by Cyrus M. Jarrett because a certain man was your father.* Then all we have to do is tell Saul and Fred, while Orrie checks the alibi, to pick up Jarrett twenty-two years ago and find out what certain man he would feel obligated to that much and that long."

"His son."

"Oh, sure. The son comes first and foremost. You stole my line. I was going to stand up and say, 'Even a baboon could feel like that about a son, and Jarrett has got one,' and walk out." I stood up. "You have Saul's number if anything happens this evening. Eugene Jarrett might drop in for a chat."

I walked out.

8

When Wolfe came down to the office from the plant rooms at eleven o'clock Friday morning, Saul Panzer ($10 an hour and worth double that), Fred Durkin ($8 an hour and worth it), and Orrie Cather ($8 an hour and usually worth it) were on three of the yellow chairs facing me, with notebooks in their hands. They had been there an hour. Saul, wiry and a little undersized all but his ears and nose, could have occupied about any spot in life that appealed to him, but he had settled for free-lance operative years ago because he could work only when he wanted to, make as much money as he needed, be outdoors a lot, and wear his old wool cap from November 1 to April 15. A reversible cap like that, light tan on one side and plaid on the other, and not there at all if you stick it in a pocket, can be a help when you're tailing. Fred, shorter than me but some broader, was apt to fool you. Just when you decided that it was too bad that some of his muscle power couldn't be traded in for brain power, he might get a wedge in where it was hard to see a crack. It *was* too bad that Orrie knew how good-looking he was. A mirror can be a handy tool, either your own or one on a wall, but not if you're more interested in checking on your hair than in the subject.

They got up when Wolfe entered, and when, after shaking hands around because he hadn't seen them for weeks, he went to his desk, they shifted their chairs to face him. I told him that they had been briefed and given expense money and that we had discussed Orrie's assignment, checking Jarrett's alibi. Wolfe looked at Saul and asked, "Comments?"

68

Saul closed his notebook. "I could make a few dozen. Who couldn't? But if we want to place her from March to October nineteen forty-four, the snag is that we don't know when she switched from Carlotta Vaughn to Elinor Denovo. To place someone that long ago is always tough, and that makes it a lot tougher."

"But you think that should be tackled first?"

"For Fred and me, yes. Of course the son is the best bet, or rather, he's the only bet as it stands now, but that's for you and Archie. McCray. Ballou told Archie that he wanted to meet you."

Wolfe tightened his lips. Paying four grown men and paying them well, or the client was, and *he* had to work. He growled. "Archie. Get Mr. McCray. I'll talk."

You would think that getting through to a vice-president would be easier and quicker than to a president, but it wasn't. Some underling positively wouldn't put Mr. McCray on until Mr. Wolfe was on, and when they were both on, voice to voice, Wolfe got clogged too. He was polite enough, saying how he would appreciate it if Mr. McCray would come at three o'clock, but McCray wasn't even sure he could come at six, and wouldn't Monday do? He wanted to get away for the weekend, but finally agreed to make it at six or a little after.

The trio stayed until lunchtime. I got a Washington call through to a three-star general at the Pentagon who hadn't forgotten something Wolfe had once done for him, strictly private, and he told Wolfe he would be glad to see Orrie Cather and give him any assistance that security would permit. Most of the hour and a half was spent on Saul's and Fred's program. All they would have were the two names and the photographs; they didn't even know if during those long-gone months she had slept among eight million others in New York or in some suburb—or even in Wisconsin. We had the names of only four people who had known her then: the Jarretts, father and son and daughter, and Bertram McCray. The daughter lived in Italy, and McCray had told me that all he knew about Elinor Denovo after she moved out of the Jarrett house was that he had seen her there three or four times during those six or seven months. It's hard to start when you have nowhere to start from. The best we could do was

three feeble stabs: Fred, with photographs, would go the
rounds of shops, from dry cleaners to drugstores, in the
neighborhood of the Jarrett houses, town and country;
Saul would try anything that occurred to him, from old
telephone directories to the charge-account records of midtown stores; and I would put an ad in all New York papers.

After lunch I did that, taking it to an agency instead
of phoning it in, because it was to be a display, not a classified, two columns wide and three inches high. Wolfe had
drafted it:

$500
will be paid for
any verifiable information
regarding the whereabouts
and movements of
CARLOTTA VAUGHN
alias
ELINOR DENOVO
between April 1, 1944
and
October 1, 1944
Box ——

Wolfe had drafted it, but not without an argument.
He wanted to make it six inches high, not three, with the
bottom half a reproduction of the three-quarters-face
photograph. My objection was that that would bring us
stacks of answers from people who would grab at any
chance to collect five hundred dollars and I would have to
spend a week or so following some of them up on a-million-
to-one odds, and a good percentage of them would develop
into pests. I won. Another objection, from Saul, not me,
was that we would be hooked by people who had seen her
in circumstances that wouldn't help, for instance, servants
who had been at Jarrett's then, but Wolfe overruled that
one. It might cost five or ten grand, but there was plenty
in the twelve savings banks. Of course another objection
was that Raymond Thorne wouldn't like it, with its public
implication that there was something about the past of

Elinor Denovo that needed to be investigated, but that was just mentioned, not argued.

At the agency, Green and Best, they said four inches high would be better than three, but I won that argument too.

It was 6:08 when Bertram McCray arrived. He looked as if he needed a weekend; his whole face was pinched, not just the corner of an eye, and his feet dragged as he walked down the hall. It's enough to wear a man out, helping to decide what to do with a couple of billion dollars' worth of other people's money. After presenting him to Wolfe and motioning him to the red leather chair, I asked if he would like to have a drink and he said no, he was going to drive eighty miles. He sat and blinked at Wolfe and said he hoped it wouldn't take long. "I don't want to be blunt," he said, "but I've had a hard week and I want some air. I didn't ask you on the phone, but I assume it's about Jarrett."

Wolfe nodded. "We've been balked. It's highly probable that he is not the father of Elinor Denovo's daughter."

"What?" McCray's mouth stayed open. "But . . . why? He sent those checks."

"Yes, that's established, thanks to Mr. Ballou and you. But the daughter was born on the twelfth of April, nineteen forty-five, so she was conceived the preceding summer, and Mr. Jarrett says he spent it abroad on a mission for the Production Allotments Board. He spent the month of July in an army hospital in Naples. He says."

"My God." McCray looked at me. "Didn't I tell you that?"

I shook my head. "And I didn't ask you. I should have, but I didn't. I apologize. So Mr. Wolfe is asking you now. Jarrett told me that he went to England in late May nineteen forty-four and then to Egypt and Italy and Africa, and came back on September sixth. We're checking it, and maybe you can help. He called me a liar. Can you call him one?"

"I can call him anything, but . . ." He looked at Wolfe. "Are you sure about the date? The birth?"

"Yes. That can't be challenged. Mr. Goodwin has seen the birth certificate."

"Then I guess we . . . you . . . my God. He was out

of the country all that summer. I can check the exact
dates he left and returned, but does that matter?"

"No. But we need to know if Elinor Denovo, then Carlotta Vaughn, was also out of the country that summer,
however briefly. Can you help on that?"

"Of course not. I didn't . . . I only saw her three or
four times after she moved out; I barely spoke to her." He
sounded peevish and looked peevish. "You could have
told me this on the phone." He looked at his watch. "An
hour wasted."

"Possibly not." Wolfe cocked his head. "You're vexed,
Mr. McCray, and so are we. Mr. Goodwin and I can't
be charged with making an unwarranted assumption. The
checks, certainly, but other circumstances too, supplied by
you—that Carlotta Vaughn left Jarrett's in the spring of
nineteen forty-four but did not end their association. It
was an acceptable conjecture that he had provided other
quarters for her if their relations had taken a course which
he preferred not to pursue in his home. We don't have
to abandon that conjecture now; we can merely adapt it.
You told Mr. Goodwin yesterday that you had once
thought it possible that something was developing between
Carlotta Vaughn and Mr. Jarrett's son. He was twenty
years of age and I presume he was away at college, but
not in the summer months, and other quarters for her could
have been provided by him. For the only son of a wealthy
man that wouldn't have been difficult. I don't need to
waste more of your time by expounding the obvious, that
the checks sent by Mr. Jarrett, if not for a daughter, might
have been for a granddaughter. I invite your opinion."

McCray was frowning. He turned the frown on me and
demanded, "Did I say that?"

I nodded. "I can repeat it to the letter if you want it."

"I don't. I must have been babbling."

"No, you weren't babbling. I was asking you about
her relations with everybody, including you, that was all.
I asked if you remembered anything specific and you
didn't."

"Of course I didn't." He turned to Wolfe. "It's ridiculous. He sent her money for twenty-two years because
his son . . . absolutely ridiculous. Anyway, there's a reason . . . No. He wouldn't . . . No." He pursed his lips,

eyed Wolfe, then me, and back at Wolfe. "I want to make one thing plain. Two things. When Mr. Ballou asked me about those checks and I learned they had been charged to Cyrus Jarrett and delivered to him, I had no objection to that information being passed to you. I was perfectly willing to supply routine information—that's all it was, routine—that would make trouble for Cyrus Jarrett. God knows he has made enough trouble for me. But I wouldn't supply information that would make trouble for his son even if I had any, and I haven't. I have high regard for Eugene Jarrett, not only as a brother officer of our bank, but as a friend. I'll tell you this—anybody could tell you this—for ten years Eugene Jarrett and his father haven't been on speaking terms. My opinion of his father is mild compared to his. Of course with him it's more personal, father and son; you know how deep that can go. If Cyrus Jarrett continued sending money to that woman—Carlotta Vaughn or Elinor Denovo—for the past ten years, it wasn't on account of his son, that's sure."

He put his palms on the chair arms and levered himself to his feet. "I'm going," he said. "You can forget Eugene Jarrett. But if I had any more information that would help with his father you'd be welcome to it. Frankly, I would like to see him get hurt, really hurt, and so would other people I could name, and he did send those checks for twenty-two years. Was it blackmail? Did she know something that *would* hurt? If so I hope you dig it up. Frankly, I would help if I could. Do you . . ." He hesitated. "If it needs any financing . . ."

"It doesn't. I have a client."

"Well, then . . ." He turned and started out, so slow, his feet dragging, that I didn't have to hurry to beat him to the hall and on to the front. At the door he thought he had something to say, but decided not to. His car, down at the curb, was a 1965 Imperial.

In the office Wolfe was pulling at his earlobe, his eyes closed. I went to my desk and sat, and said, "If you want my opinion, we wasted not only his time but ours too. I don't buy his slant on the son, even if they hate each other's guts. His obligation was to the mother, not the father. Damn it, it's got to be the son. Who else?"

He grunted and his eyes opened. "What if our basic assumption is false? What if the payments had no connection with the birth?"

"We're sunk. We bow out. But in that case there wasn't just one lie in Elinor's letter, the whole damn letter was a lie, and I don't believe it. If the payments had nothing to do with Amy, why did Elinor keep it, every century of it, for her?"

"Women are random clusters of vagaries."

"Who said that?"

"I did."

"Not that random."

His shoulders went up and down. "Have you time for a letter before you leave? To be mailed now?"

"No. But I might as well start making up for the boner I pulled." I got my office notebook from a drawer. "Miss Rowan will feed me no matter what time I come. She's the understanding type."

"Pfui." He would never forget the time she had called him Pete and he had had Houri de Perse perfume sprinkled on him. "Have you Eugene Jarrett's home address?"

I nodded. "I got it this morning. I thought Saul might need it."

"To him at his home, special delivery. *Dear Mr. Jarrett: On behalf of a client I need information regarding the activities and associates of Miss Carlotta Vaughn during the years nineteen forty-three and nineteen forty-four, comma, when she was in your father's employ, comma, and I have been told that you may be able to supply some details. Period. I shall appreciate it if you will kindly call at my office, comma, at the above address, comma, on Monday, comma, at eleven in the morning, comma, or at either two-thirty or six in the afternoon. Period. I hope that one of those hours will be convenient for you. Sincerely yours.*"

"Why not offer him nine in the evening too?"

"As you know, I don't like to work after dinner. But I suppose . . . Very well. Add it."

I pulled the typewriter around and got out paper and carbon.

An hour later, as I headed north on the Henry Hudson Parkway, keeping to sixty, I wasn't on a perch either professionally or personally. Professionally, the client was being neglected. I had phoned her Friday morning that it was very unlikely that Jarrett was her father, and told her why, and that was all. She deserved to know that she had been right about Denovo, that her mother's real name was Carlotta Vaughn; at least we could give her that for the eight days we had been on it. Personally, there I was bound for a swimming pool in a glade while Orrie was in Washington digging into army records and Saul and Fred were poking into holes that were probably empty. I should have been doing something brilliant, like finding a mattress somewhere with hairs from two human heads on it which a scientist would prove had been left there by Carlotta Vaughn, alias Elinor Denovo, and Eugene Jarrett.

I wasn't feeling any better as I drove back to town Sunday evening. The weekend had been messy. There is never more than one house guest besides me; it may be anybody from a female poet to a cowboy from the Montana ranch Lily owns; and that time it was Amy Denovo. She gave it a good start only an hour after I arrived. She called me Archie. We were on the terrace. I had finished off the steak Mimi had broiled—they had eaten—and was forking the blueberry pie when Amy got out a cigarette and I lit it, and she said, "Thank you, Archie." Of course Lily didn't bat an eye; she wouldn't. But as far as she knew Amy had seen me only three times for a total of about nine minutes, and she didn't have to be a cluster of vagaries to wonder what the score was. Was Amy just being flip, or had I decided to see more of her, not at the penthouse, and taken steps? I couldn't tell her what Miss Denovo had hired Wolfe to do, so I skipped it. But it was there in the air. Between Lily and me it was thoroughly understood that what I did was none of her business unless it touched her—and, naturally, vice versa—but the fact that I had met Miss Denovo at the penthouse put it on the borderline. So it didn't help the weekend.

A couple of other things didn't help either. One of the five guests for lunch Saturday was a woman with a green wig who had positive inside information that President Johnson and Dean Rusk had decided three years ago to kill everybody in China with hydrogen bombs, and that was the real reason for what they were doing in Vietnam.

Of course the only thing to do with such a clunk is to ignore him or her, but she kept it up so loud and long that I finally told her that I had positive inside information that Senator Fulbright had once had an affair with one of Ho Chi Minh's concubines, and that was the real reason he wanted the bombing stopped. That was a mistake. The idea appealed to her and she wanted all the details.

And Sunday afternoon some uninvited people dropped in—a couple I had met there before who had a place over beyond Bedford Village. They weren't so bad, but they had a guy with them who they said had talked them into coming because he wanted to meet me. His name was Floyd Vance and he said he was a public-relations counselor. Evidently he wanted to meet me because he wanted to meet Nero Wolfe. He was drumming up trade. He said that if anybody needed expert handling of his public image a private detective did, and he would like very much to create a presentation to propose to Nero Wolfe. He also said that if we were working on a case and I would tell him about it, he could use that as a basis for the presentation. When he said that I sharpened my eyes and ears a little, and my tongue, thinking he might be making a stab at detective work himself for somebody, for instance Cyrus M. Jarrett, but decided he was just another character who was so dedicated to improving other people's images that he had no time left for his own. I met one once who—no, that's enough for that weekend.

So as I said, I wasn't feeling any better as I drove back to town. Sometimes it's things that take the joy out of life, like a blowout when you're hitting sixty or a button coming off of a shirt when you're in a hurry, but usually it's people. Of course, of the three people who had made that weekend less than perfect Amy was the only one whose contribution would carry over. Lily would do some wondering for a week or so—who wouldn't?—but I certainly wasn't going to explain. When two people who want to get along start needing to have things explained, look out. I would tell the client about her mother's real name when I felt like it.

9

The trouble with putting a box number on an ad instead of your name and address and phone number, especially if it's in three papers, is getting the replies. Phoning at ten o'clock Monday morning and learning that there were some, I went for them, got two at the *Times* and four at the *Gazette,* opened them there, and found them so screwy that I bothered to take them home only because I always keep everything connected with a job until it's finished. One was from a man who said Carlotta Vaughn was his grandmother, and maybe a Carlotta Vaughn was, but he didn't mention Elinor Denovo.

When I got back a little after eleven Fritz said there had been no calls, but as I entered the office the phone rang and I crossed to my desk, nodding to Wolfe on the way, and got it.

"Nero Wolfe's office, Archie Goodwin speaking."

Female voice: "Good morning. Mr. Jarrett would like to speak to Mr. Wolfe."

"Good morning. Please put Mr. Jarrett on."

"Is Mr. Wolfe there?"

"Yes."

"Please put him on."

"Now listen." I motioned to Wolfe. "Last Friday I got Mr. McCray for Mr. Wolfe and I was forced to put Mr. Wolfe on first. You can't have it coming and going. Put Mr. Jarrett on or I hang up."

"May I have your name, please?"

"Archie Goodwin."

"Please hold the wire, Mr. Goodwin."

77

I timed it: two minutes and twenty seconds. Wolfe had his phone.

"Eugene Jarrett speaking. Nero Wolfe?"

Me: "Please hold the wire, Mr. Jarrett."

Wolfe should have waited at least a minute, but he hates the phone, either holding or talking. "This is Nero Wolfe. Yes, Mr. Jarrett?"

"I have your letter. I'll come around six."

"Good. As I said in the letter, I'll appreciate it. I'll expect you."

They hung up together. There was a case where the approach took five minutes and the meet about ten seconds. A piece by a scientist in the Sunday *New York Times Magazine* which I had read during the weekend had explained why this is the age of instant communication.

There were some items in the morning mail that needed attention, or at least got it, but we were interrupted a few times by phone calls: from Saul, who had drawn nothing but blanks; from Fred, who had found three people who had recognized the photographs but hadn't been any help; and from Orrie, from Washington, who had verified most of Jarrett's places and dates and was working on the rest. The hospital part, which covered most of July, was airtight. You are probably thinking that the client was getting damned little for her money, and I agree. When I returned from a trip to the mailbox at the corner it was lunchtime, and as we crossed to the dining room Wolfe said something about Mr. Cramer and I asked if he had phoned. Wolfe said no, he had come, late Saturday afternoon.

I was sorry I had missed it because talk by those two is always worth hearing. You get good examples of how much a man can say in a few words and also of how little he can say in a lot of words. So back in the office after lunch I said I would just as soon know what Cramer had wanted, and Wolfe said only what he always wanted, information; he had said nothing that would help us any.

I settled back and crossed my legs. "I haven't kept count," I said, "but at least a thousand times I have given you a verbatim report of a conversation. I can't tell you o because I don't pay you, you pay me, but I can suggest t. I am suggesting it."

A corner of his mouth went up a sixteenth of an inch. For him it was a broad smile. "My memory is as good as yours, Archie."

"Then it would be no strain. I said verbatim."

"I know you did." He squinted at me. "Well . . . Mr. Cramer, admitted by Fritz, arrived shortly after six o'clock. We ex—"

"The exact time?"

"I don't have it on my wrist, as you do. We exchanged greetings and he sat.

"Cramer: 'Where's Goodwin?'

"Wolfe: 'Not here, as you see.'

"Cramer: 'Yeah. I doubt if there's a man on earth as good at fielding questions as you are. So I'll ask another one. Saturday the nineteenth, a week ago, Goodwin rang Sergeant Stebbins and asked him about a hit-and-run three months ago that killed a woman named Elinor Denovo. Some crap about you and him discussing crime. Last Monday morning, I came and asked Goodwin why he had called Stebbins. He said he knew nothing about that hit-and-run except what he had read in the papers, and neither did you, and you hadn't been consulted about it, and your only client was a girl who wanted to find her father. I want the name of that girl. I wish Goodwin was here. Where is he?'

"Wolfe: 'Absent. Mr. Cramer. You may query me in that tone only when your questions are justified by your official function.'

"Cramer: 'Okay, I'll ask one that *is* justified. If you haven't been consulted about that hit-and-run why do you offer to pay five hundred dollars for information about Elinor Denovo? That also justifies my question about the girl—and about Goodwin. He told me a goddam lie.'

"Wolfe: 'No. I can repeat now what he told you a week ago, and I do, and it is true. I—'"

He broke off and demanded, "How the devil did he know that advertisement was mine?"

I turned my palms up. "Someone on some newspaper did a favor for some cop. If I find out who, you can write a letter to the publisher."

"Pah. To resume:

"Wolfe: '. . . and it is true. I am not investigating that hit-and-run. My client's concern with Elinor Denovo relates not to her death but to her life. You should have inferred that from the advertisement; it asks for information, not about her last day or even her last year, but about many years ago. The information—'

"Cramer: 'Who is Carlotta Vaughn?'

"Wolfe: 'You're not in good form, Mr. Cramer. The advertisement makes it obvious that Carlotta Vaughn is, or was, Elinor Denovo. The information my client has given me is confidential and has no bearing on the hit-and-run.'

"Cramer: 'You don't know that. When I'm investigating a homicide *I* decide what has a bearing and what hasn't.'

"Wolfe: 'Must we repeat ourselves? Must I remind you again that until events answer that question conclusively my judgment, for which I alone am responsible, need not bow to yours—nor yours to mine? Am I withholding information from an officer of the law? Yes. Is it pertinent to his investigation of a crime? No. You have never made me change that no to a yes. Do that and you'll have me.'

"Cramer: 'By God, I will. Some day I will.' "

Wolfe waved a hand toward the hall, waving Cramer out. "Next time I'll turn the recorder on. Questions."

I uncrossed my legs and straightened up. "No questions, just two comments. First, I think you left out a word or two, particularly one that he often uses. That's censorship, which you condemn. Second, there's something about that hit-and-run that makes it special, and it would be nice to know what it is. Cramer wouldn't be bothering personally about a three-month-old hit-and-run, even with you interested in the victim, unless it had some special kink. Maybe a hot lead that fizzled out—anyway, something. But as you said, it's her life we're working on, not her death. Thank you for the report. Satisfactory."

He pushed a button, two short and one long, for beer.

I spent most of the next three hours finding out next to nothing about Eugene Jarrett. He wasn't in *Who's Who,* and since there was no other likely source of information about him in the office I went for a walk, keeping on the shady side of the street. There were just four items about him in the *Gazette* morgue, and the only two worth an entry in my notebook were that he had married a girl named Adele Baldwin on November 18, 1951, and he had become a vice-president of Seaboard Bank and Trust Company in December 1959. Lon Cohen knew absolutely nothing about him, and neither did a couple of others on the *Gazette* that he got on the phone. On the way out I stopped at the sixteenth floor to see if there were any more replies to the ad and got two that were more of the same.

At the *Times* there was another reply, also impossible, and nothing in the morgue about Eugene Jarrett except such routine facts as that he graduated from Harvard in 1945 and he had been a sponsor of a dinner to honor somebody in 1963. The biggest blank was the New York public library, where I got stubborn and spent a full hour. You wouldn't believe that after all that expert research I didn't even know whether that vice-president of the third largest bank in New York had any children or not, when I returned to the old brownstone a little before six o'clock. But I didn't. I had supposed, when I left, that I would have to get back in time to go up to the plant rooms to brief Wolfe on him before he came, but it wasn't even worth buzzing him on the house phone. When he came down I told him that we would learn more about Eugene Jarrett in one glance at him than I had learned all afternoon, and the doorbell rang.

I was right, too. What I learned looking at him, as I let him in and escorted him to the office and got him seated in the red leather chair, may have been irrelevant and immaterial, but at least it was definite. If a vice-president of a big bank is supposed to do any work, he didn't belong there. There was no resemblance to his father at all, especially the eyes. His were gray-blue too, but even when they were aimed straight at you, you had the feeling that they were seeing something else, maybe a ship he wanted to be on or a pretty girl sitting on a cloud. I don't often have fancy ideas, so that shows you the effect those eyes had. It would be dumb to expect a man like that to do any work. The rest of him was normal enough—about my height, square-shouldered, an ordinary face. Seated, he ignored Wolfe and me while his eyes took their time to go around the room. Apparently they liked the rug, but they stayed longest on the globe over by the bookshelves. Not many people coming there have seen a globe as big as that one, 35½ inches in diameter.

He finally turned the eyes on Wolfe and said, "A fascinating occupation, yours, Mr. Wolfe. People come to you for answers as they did to the Pythia at Delphi or the Clarian prophet. But of course you make no claim to mantic divination. That is now only for charlatans. What are you, a scientist, or an artist?"

Wolfe was frowning at him. "If you please, Mr. Jarrett, no labels. Labels are for the things men make, not for men. The most primitive man is too complex to be labeled. Do *you* have one?"

"No. But I can label any man whose faculties are concentrated on a single purpose. I can label Charles de Gaulle or Robert Welch or Stokely Carmichael."

"If you do, don't glue them on, and have replacements handy."

Jarrett nodded. "Nothing is unalterable, not even a label. I have altered mine for my father several times. I mention him because it is apropos. The only reference to him in your letter was that Carlotta Vaughn was in his employ, but Bert McCray has told me about your poke at him and how he met it. He has also told me of your intention to transfer the poke to me. I would enjoy discussing my father with you—we might get a better label for him than the one I have—but your letter asks about Carlotta Vaughn. First we should dispose of me. You thought my father was the father of a child she bore, were confronted with evidence that he wasn't, and decided that I was. Is that correct?"

"Not 'decided.' Conjectured or surmised—or even inferred."

"No matter. You're in for another disappointment. When Bert McCray told me about it Saturday, and then when your letter came, I decided to save you time and expense —and of course avoid annoyance for myself—by telling you something that many people conjecture or surmise but only a few really know. But I realized that my telling you wouldn't settle it for you, so this morning I phoned my doctor."

He turned to me. "You're Archie Goodwin?"

I told him yes. He got a leather case from his pocket, fingered a card out, and extended his hand, and I went and took the card. The "James Odell Worthington, M.D." might actually have been engraved.

"Dr. Worthington will see you at nine tomorrow morning," Jarrett said. "Be on time; he's a very busy man. He will tell you that I am incapable of impregnating a woman and always have been. He has a reputation and would on no account risk it by telling you that if there was any remote possibility that you would ever prove him wrong."

He turned to Wolfe. "Your letter said that you want information about Carlotta Vaughn."

I would have told him to go climb a tree. Wolfe probably would have liked to, but the only visible sign was the tip of his forefinger making a little circle on the desk blotter. He asked, "Did Dr. Worthington know you in nineteen forty-four?"

"Yes, he was one of the doctors who had tried to save my mother. He's an internist and the cancer specialists had taken charge, but my mother depended on him. Don't ask me, ask him." He brushed it aside. "Ask me anything you want to about Carlotta Vaughn, but I doubt if I know anything that will help. She changed her name to Elinor Denovo, and she had a daughter now twenty-two years old, and during those twenty-two years my father sent her a check for a thousand dollars every month. Is that the situation?"

"Yes."

"Then I need a new label for him. This is fantastic. It doesn't fit anything I thought I knew about him. Not that he would ignore a responsibility; he fulfills any and all responsibilities; but *he* decides when he is responsible and when he isn't. He certainly wouldn't have felt responsible if I had impregnated Carlotta Vaughn or any other woman, or a dozen. Bert McCray thinks it was blackmail, but it wasn't. It's inconceivable that he has ever submitted to blackmail by anybody for anything. It's fascinating. I understand from Avery Ballou that this Elinor Denovo is dead, but didn't she ever tell anyone what the money was for?"

"While alive, no. But a letter opened by her daughter after her death said *this money is from your father*. And again, *this money came from your father*. Mr. Goodwin and I see no reason to question it."

"Fantastic. Unbelievable." Jarrett narrowed his eyes to slits, put his elbows on the chair arms, and rubbed his left palm with his right. Then he came up and was on his feet. "I'm no good sitting down." He moved, across to the bookshelves and looked at titles, then to the globe and rotated it, slowly, twice around. He came and stood in the center of the room, looking down at me as if I were a pretty girl on a cloud, then turned to Wolfe. "I don't do anything at the bank, you know. I know nothing about banking. But they don't keep me and pay me only because my father owns stock that he won't sell. They say I have insight. I don't know what to call it, I can't label *that*, but I do sometimes see things that they have not seen. I have never tried to force it, and I'm not going to try to force this, but I want to see it more than I have ever wanted to see anything. *My father!*"

He went to the red leather chair and sat. "It would be pointless to ask me anything about Carlotta Vaughn. Bert McCray told me that her child was conceived in the summer of nineteen forty-four. I had been rejected by the army and spent that summer working in a war-materials plant in California. I know nothing that could possibly help you." He got up again. "Come and have dinner with me." He looked at me. "You too. Sometimes it helps to have people around, I don't know why."

"I doubt," Wolfe said, "if it would help to have Mr. Goodwin and me around. We're in a pickle. I wrote you that I would appreciate it if you would call at my office. I retract that. I don't appreciate it at all."

"I suppose not." He turned and sort of wandered toward the hall, but stopped and swung around. "The pickle you're in is nothing to mine. I thought I had my father plain and clear, and now this! I'm going to see it—I don't know when, but I will. I have to."

I had circled around him and was in the hall, but he didn't see me as he came to the front, where I had the door open. I shut the door after him, returned to the office, and stood looking down at Wolfe. With his chin down he had to have his eyes wide open to glare at the globe. After ten seconds of that he raised his head to growl at me. "Sit down. Confound it, you know I like eyes at a level."

"Yeah. Shall I get the darts out?"

"No. How much have we spent?"

That was dangerous. That question meant, If I return the retainer and drop it, how much am I out? That hadn't happened often, but it wasn't unthinkable. I went to my chair and sat. "I admit," I said, "that we've never had a tougher one, and it may be too tough even for you, but why can't we just hang on until Eugene sees it? He'll tell us, and we'll check it and hand it to the client, and she'll think—"

"Shut up!"

That was better. There wasn't going to be a battle about quitting. He scowled at me and demanded, "Do we abandon that wretch?"

I thought that was hitting below the belt, to call a vice-president a wretch just because he couldn't impregnate a woman. "Yes," I said, "any odds you want. Of course I'll see that doctor, but we might as well cross him off now."

"Do we also abandon Mr. McCray?"

I grinned at him. Even in that pickle, that called for a grin. "I'm right with you," I said. "We have never considered McCray; we were considering only Jarretts. You were considering McCray for the first time when I went to let that wretch out, and so was I. He is our only source for the fact that the checks were charged to Cyrus M. Jarrett. We have had no corroboration of it. Might they have been actually charged to McCray? Certainly. Might he have had opportunities to impregnate Carlotta Vaughn during the summer of nineteen forty-four? Certainly. But in that case, Jarrett knew nothing about the checks, and why didn't he just kick me out?"

I waved a hand. "I reported it verbatim. Jarrett said, 'Those checks are in the files of the Seaboard Bank and Trust Company. Who told you about them?' The next day, Thursday, why did the name Carlotta Vaughn, just the name, get me to him? Why was he ready with those places and dates for that summer? His whole reaction, everything he said." I shook my head. "The checks came from Cyrus M. Jarrett. Since you had a good two minutes to consider McCray I'm surprised that you bothered to mention him."

"You saw Mr. Jarrett and I didn't."

"And I have no desire to see him again. Forget McCray."

"Then we're left with nothing."

"We have Saul and Fred and Orrie. And me. And, oh, yes, excuse me, we have you."

He looked at his current book, always there on the desk, picked it up, dropped it, and glared at me.

10

Sixty-eight hours later, at three o'clock Thursday afternoon, Wolfe and I sat in the office with nothing more to say. We still had exactly what we had had Monday at dinnertime, five detectives, counting us.

First, to finish off Eugene Jarrett. At 8:50 Tuesday morning I had got off the elevator at the tenth floor of a building on Park Avenue in the Eighties, given my name to a woman at a desk, and been sent to a big old-fashioned room with twenty chairs distributed around the walls and tables, eight or nine of them occupied by people who didn't look very gay, which wasn't too discouraging because the names of four M.D.s had been on the plaque. At 9:20 another woman had come and ushered me down a hall to a door which she opened. When I entered, a gray-haired man with shaggy black eyebrows and a tired wide mouth, at a desk, writing on a pad, nodded and pointed to a chair, went on writing for a couple of minutes, and then put the pen down and turned to me. He asked if my name was Archie Goodwin and I said yes, and he said that since the information he was to give me was confidential he would like to be sure. . . .

I got my wallet out and showed him things, and he nodded and looked at his wristwatch. "We squeezed you in," he said, "because Mr. Jarrett said it was urgent. He asked me to confirm his statement to you that he is sterile and has been sterile all his adult life. Very well, I do. That is true."

"If you don't mind," I said, "we want it airtight. That's of your personal knowledge? Not hearsay?"

"I wouldn't make such a statement from hearsay. My *professional* knowledge, yes. Four examinations and analyses, at intervals, in seventeen years. Not only is the sperm count per se too low, but also the percentage of abnormal forms is too high. It is conclusive."

"Thank you. Seventeen years ago was nineteen fifty. What about earlier? Say nineteen forty-four."

He shook his head. "Extremely unlikely. I would accept it as a possibility only on incontrovertible evidence, and even then with reluctance. I have known the family for nearly thirty years, since nineteen forty. If Eugene Jarrett was fertile in nineteen forty-four only certain infections—mumps is the commonest one—could have caused his present condition, and he has had none of them." He looked at his watch. "Mr. Jarrett didn't tell me what this is about. If it's a paternity suit it's ridiculous. I would be glad to testify."

I thanked him again and went. So much for Eugene Jarrett. But on the way home I stopped in at Doc Vollmer's office, in a house he owns on the same block as the old brownstone, and asked him about the reputation of James Odell Worthington, M.D., and sperm counts and abnormal forms and mumps; and that did finish off Eugene Jarrett.

Cyrus M. Jarrett was finished too, on Wednesday, when Orrie came back from Washington with three notebooks full of details from official records. The places and dates as Jarrett had rattled them off to me all checked, and if he had taken a day off to fly across the Atlantic on a personal errand off the record, where did he get an airplane in wartime?

After dinner Monday evening I had made a trip uptown and spent a couple of hours with the client. The news that her mother's real name was Carlotta Vaughn and that she had come from Wisconsin didn't impress her much; as she had said, she had known her mother all her life. Also, she wasn't too impressed by the news that we had eliminated the Jarretts; she wasn't interested in men who were *not* her father; what she was after was the man who *was* her father. I made it plain that we were no longer turning over stones, we were trying to find a stone to turn, and it was anybody's guess how long it would take. She said she should have taken my bet a week ago when

I offered her even money that we would spot her father within three days.

Saul and Fred had kept at their hunt for stones until Tuesday noon, but had been called in when I got seven more replies to the ad and three of them were worth a look. Saul took one, from a shoe-repair man on West Fifty-fourth Street who wrote that Carlotta Vaughn had been a customer of his for several months in 1944. I got his letter at the *News*. When Saul went to see him, he took along photographs of six other young women, and the shoeman picked Carlotta Vaughn at the first look. He knew nothing of any Elinor Denovo, but he remembered it was during the summer of 1944 that Carlotta Vaughn had been a regular customer for both repairs and shines, because it was that August that his son had been killed in action in France. He couldn't say when he had seen her last, but thought it had been late summer or early fall. He didn't think he had ever had her address, but if so it was gone now. Of course she had probably lived nearby, and after shelling out five hundred dollars to the shoeman, Saul had gone to work on the neighborhood.

A reply I got at the *Times* was from a woman who had been a clerk at Altman's in 1944 and was now at a nursing home in Fairfield County. Fred took her, and found her so vague that after twenty-four hours he was still trying to find out how she knew that a customer she had waited on several times was named Carlotta Vaughn, since there was no record of any deliveries ever made to her. But she, too, had picked Carlotta Vaughn out of seven pictures, so she got her five centuries.

The third reply that seemed possible, which I got at the *Gazette,* was from a man named Salvatore Manzoni. I took him. He had been a waiter at Sardi's for fifteen years and still was. In 1944 he had been a waiter at Tufitti's, a restaurant on East Forty-sixth Street which had folded in 1949, and Carlotta Vaughn had dined at one of his tables two or three times a week for several months in 1944. He spotted her picture instantly, and he knew her name was Carlotta Vaughn because she had often reserved a table. What made Salvatore Manzoni a real find was that he had probably actually seen Amy's father in the flesh, not once but many times, for Carlotta Vaughn

had always had a male companion, and always the same
one. When I heard that, I had a tingle at the bottom of
my spine; by God, I was going to get the name, then and
there. But I didn't. It wasn't that Salvatore Manzoni
couldn't remember it; he had never known it. As far as
he knew, a reservation had never been made under the
man's name. Possibly it might have been known to someone else at the restaurant, perhaps the owner and manag-
er, Giuseppe Tufitti, who might or might not be still alive.

A description by anyone of a man he saw last week
will never make you really see him, and 1944 was twenty-three years ago, and this subject had been mostly sitting
at a table when he was under Salvatore Manzoni's eyes,
which makes a difference. What I got was: age, early
thirties. Height, around six feet. Weight, around a hundred
and seventy. Shoulders, maybe square, maybe rounded a
little. Head, a little bigger than average. Face, not round,
maybe rather long; not pale, maybe a little tanned. Hair,
dark brown. Eyes, brown (just a guess). Nose and mouth
and ears and chin, yes, he had them.

If that really shows him to you, you have better sight
than I have. It did exclude the Jarretts and Bertram Mc-
Cray, but they were already out. I wish I knew if you
would really be interested in what we did during the next
forty-eight hours. I doubt it, because it was all negative.
Wednesday morning Saul and Fred had been put on it
too, and also Orrie when he returned from Washington. If
we could name and place Carlotta Vaughn's dinner partner
for those months of 1944 it was 20 to 1 that we would
have Amy's father, which was the job, and we gave it all
we had. Detecting can be fun, but it can be a pain not
only in the neck but also in the head, the guts, the back,
the legs, the feet, and the ass. And often is. It was that
time.

So at three o'clock Thursday afternoon Wolfe and I sat
in the office with nothing more to say. Saul and Fred and
Orrie were still out pecking at it, but when they called in
we wouldn't be disappointed because we were expecting
nothing. Wolfe had started his second bottle of beer since
lunch, which exceeded his quota, and I had just returned
from the kitchen with a slug of Irish, which made me a
lush trying to drown it. I looked at Wolfe, who had his

eyes closed and his jaw clamped, and said, "If you're trying to figure how much you're out, it's three grand plus, not counting me."

He shook his head but didn't open his eyes. "I am making assumptions. I am assuming that Miss Denovo's father murdered her mother; that it is more feasible to find him as a murderer than as a father, since he became a father twenty-two years ago and became a murderer only three months ago; that some recent event supplied the motive for the murder; and that the most likely person to have knowledge of that event is Raymond Thorne or someone in his employ who was closely associated with Elinor Denovo." His eyes opened. "I'll start with Mr. Thorne."

I put the glass with what was left of the Irish on my desk. "Holy heaven. That's the wildest goose you ever chased."

"Perhaps. Sitting here hour after hour and day after day getting futile reports from you and Saul and Fred and Orrie is affecting my appetite and my palate. This morning I had to read a page twice. Intolerable. Can you have Mr. Thorne here at six o'clock?"

"I can try. Is this just a spasm or do you mean it?"

"I don't have spasms."

"We can discuss that some other time. I have a suggestion. You may remember my saying Monday afternoon that Cramer wouldn't be bothering about a three-months-old hit-and-run unless it had some special kink. It might help to know what it is. I request permission to go and ask him."

"Why should he tell you?"

"Leave that, quoting you, to my intelligence guided by experience."

"You can't give him the client's name."

"Certainly not. But he probably knows it, after that ad."

"Very well. First, Mr. Thorne."

It took nearly an hour to get Raymond Thorne because he was somewhere watching TV cameras make a Raymond Thorne production, and when I finally had him he said he couldn't possibly make it at six o'clock. I reminded him that he had told me he would like to help Amy any way he could, and he said he would come at nine. Getting Inspector Cramer was easier and quicker. He was at his office and would see me. Wolfe had gone up to the plant rooms and I went to the kitchen to tell Fritz I was leaving.

The cop at the top of Homicide South could surely have had a bigger room and a bigger desk and better chairs for visitors than the setup on West Twentieth Street, but Cramer liked to stick to things he was used to, including that old felt hat, which was always there on a corner of his desk when it wasn't on his head, although there was a rack only a step away. I sat on the wooden chair at the end of his desk while he finished with a folder he was going through. When he closed it and turned to me, I said, "I bring hot news. We're working on that hit-and-run. Mr. Wolfe thought we should tell you because we said we weren't."

He put on an act. He demanded, "What hit-and-run?"

"On May twenty-sixth, nineteen sixty-seven, a woman named Elinor Denovo was crossing Eighty-second Street and—"

"Oh, yes. So you're working on it. So Wolfe wants to know something, so he sends you. He can go to hell."

I nodded. "So you would like to know what he wants to know, so you let me in when you're busy. I'll make it brief and answer questions within reason. What we told you was the truth and the whole truth: our only client was and is a woman who wants us to find her father, whom she has never seen. She doesn't know who or what he was or is, and she wants to. We have smoked out three different Grade A leads, but they have all fizzled. Two full weeks, and we have a load of nothing, either for the client or for you. So an hour ago Mr. Wolfe decided that it's easier to find a murderer than a father, therefore the father was the murderer. As you know, that isn't how his mind usually works, but this isn't his mind working, it's a spasm, though he says he doesn't have spasms. It's just that his appetite is letting him down and he's desperate, and he pays me and I have to humor him when he sends me on a sappy errand. I would like to buy a fact. If there is any interesting fact about that hit-and-run that hasn't been published and you'll tell me what it is, off the record, I am authorized to give you Mr. Wolfe's word of honor that if we get anything you might be able to use we'll pass it on to you before we make any use of it our-

Introducing the first and only complete hardcover collection of Agatha Christie's mysteries

Now you can enjoy the
greatest mysteries ever written
in a magnificent
Home Library Edition.

Discover Agatha Christie's world of mystery, adventure and intrigue

Agatha Christie's timeless tales of mystery and suspense offer something for every reader—mystery fan or not—young and old alike. And now, you can build a complete hardcover library of her world-famous mysteries by subscribing to <u>The Agatha Christie Mystery Collection.</u>

This exciting Collection is your passport to a world where mystery reigns supreme. Volume after volume, you and your family will enjoy mystery reading at its very best.

You'll meet Agatha Christie's world-famous detectives like Hercule Poirot, Jane Marple, and the likeable Tommy and Tuppence Beresford.

In your readings, you'll visit Egypt, Paris, England and other exciting destinations where murder is always on the itinerary. And wherever you travel, you'll become deeply involved in some of the most ingenious and diabolical plots ever invented ... "cliff-hangers" that only Dame Agatha could create!

It all adds up to mystery reading that's so good ... it's almost criminal. And it's yours every month with <u>The Agatha Christie Mystery Collection.</u>

Solve the greatest mysteries of all time. The Collection contains all of Agatha Christie's classic works including *Murder on the Orient Express, Death on the Nile, And Then There Were None, The ABC Murders* and her ever-popular whodunit, *The Murder of Roger Ackroyd.*

Each handsome hardcover volume is Smythe sewn and printed on high quality acid-free paper so it can withstand even the most murderous treatment. Bound in Sussex-blue simulated leather with gold titling, <u>The Agatha Christie Mystery Collection</u> will make a tasteful addition to your living room, or den.

selves. At least two minutes before. I'd offer my word of honor too, only I'm not sure you think I have one. Questions."

He picked up a phone transmitter, in a moment told it, "Coffee," replaced it, and swiveled his chair to face me without twisting his thick neck. "We haven't bothered with Amy Denovo," he said. "After that ad of course we knew she was Wolfe's client, but we had pumped her good in June. The father angle didn't help us any unless she found him and maybe not then. You say you haven't? Found him?"

"We haven't got even a smell. But you came to see me and you phoned Mr. Wolfe."

"You had phoned Stebbins. You know damned well that when I find Wolfe within a mile I smell a rat. I thought—"

"Do I tell him you called him a rat?"

"You do not. He's a lot of things I can name, but he's not a rat. I thought he might be able to name a man who smokes a certain kind of cigar."

"I know one who smokes Monte Cristos. He gets them from a purser on a ship."

"Yeah. You'll clown while they're embalming you. If you want an interesting fact off the record, we've got one we've been saving, but hell, we might as well put it on television. We've got nine fingerprints of that hit-and-run driver, and six of them are as good as you could want."

The door opened and a uniformed city employee entered, came, and put an old scarred wooden tray on Cramer's desk blotter. As Cramer nodded thanks and picked up the pot to pour, I asked, "Didn't the damn fool ever hear of gloves?"

He put the pot down. "They weren't on the car. On the floor, in front, was a leather cigar case. He got it out to light one while he was parked on Second Avenue waiting for her, and there she came, and he dropped it on the seat . . ."

My brows were up. "You're saying it was first-degree."

He took a healthy swallow of coffee. I have to sip when it's that hot. "Wolfe is," he said, "not me. I was doing him a favor, reconstructing it for him. I don't give a damn how he happened to leave it; we've got it. But we can't

match the prints—here, Washington, London—nowhere.
There were two cigars in the case. Gold Label Bonitas.
Knowing, as I do, the kind of stunts Wolfe is capable of,
it was possible he was getting set to ask me if I would
care to meet a man who smoked Gold Label Bonitas and
was shy a case to carry them in." He drank coffee.

"If the case is handy," I said, "I would enjoy looking
at it. So I could describe it to Mr. Wolfe."

"It's at the laboratory. It's polished black calfskin, not
new but not worn much, stamped on the inside 'Corwin
Deluxe.' No other marks. Nothing special about it to
trace."

"I suppose the woman who owned the car—"

The door was opening and a cop stepped in. Cramer
asked him, "Yes?" and he said Sergeant So-and-so had
arrived with What's-his-name, and I stood up. It would
have been a dumb remark anyway. They have some
darned smart dicks at Homicide South, and one of them
had certainly asked the owner of the car if the cigar case
was hers.

11

Raymond Thorne was more than half an hour late. It was 9:40 when the doorbell rang and I went and admitted him, took him to the office, introduced him, nodded him to the red leather chair, asked him what he would like to drink, and went to the kitchen to fill his order for brandy and a glass of water.

When the three 'teers had phoned in with their usual reports, nothing, they had been told to call at nine in the morning. They were the three 'teers because once at a conference Orrie had said they were the three musketeers and we had tried to change it to fit. We tried snoopeteers, privateers (for private eyes), dicketeers, wolfeteers, hawketeers, and others, and ended up by deciding that none of them was good enough and settling for the three 'teers. They had not been told that we were now looking for a murderer, not just a father; I saved that for morning so they would get a good night's sleep.

On the way back from Twentieth Street I had found a cigar counter with a box of Gold Label Bonitas, the third counter I tried, and had bought a couple—two for sixty-five cents—and Wolfe and I had given them a good look. A Gold Label Bonita is four and three-quarters inches long, medium thick, and medium blunt at both ends. It comes in a cellophane tube, and its label says Gold Label but not Bonita. The Bonita is only on the box. I lit one and took a few puffs, but neither Wolfe nor I would claim that if we entered a room where a man had recently smoked a cigar we could testify under oath that it had been a Gold Label Bonita. It did taste and smell like tobacco smoke, which is more than I can say for the—

but he may read this. I dropped the other one in a drawer and gave Wolfe a full account of my conversation with Raymond Thorne ten days earlier, which I had never reported verbatim.

Thorne's first remark after a sip of brandy was that a close-up of Wolfe there in his chair, with sprays of orchids scattered over the desk, would make a marvelous shot for a one-minute commercial. He said that of course he didn't make many commercials, but a friend of his did, and what a picture! Wolfe had to rub his lips with a knuckle to stop the words that wanted out. Thorne was going to help him find a murderer, or he hoped he was.

"My friend would be glad to come and discuss it with you," Thorne said.

"That can wait," Wolfe said. "I'm fully occupied with the job I'm on. On behalf of Miss Denovo, I thank you for coming. I know you told Mr. Goodwin that you could supply no information that would help, but it is a common occurrence for a man to have knowledge of a fact and to be quite unaware of its significance. I once questioned a young woman for three days on what she regarded as irrelevant trivialities, and finally got a fact that exposed a murderer."

"I'm afraid I can't spare three days." Thorne took a sip of brandy and stirred it in his mouth with his tongue. "This cognac is marvelous. Speaking of facts, evidently you knew one I didn't, from that ad . . . I suppose that ad in the *Times* was yours?"

"Yes."

"*Alias* Elinor Denovo. Carlotta something *alias* Elinor Denovo. Why the 'alias' if Denovo was her married name? Her daughter's name is Amy Denovo."

"That's one of the complications, Mr. Thorne. A client's communications with a detective she has hired are not legally privileged, but they are often confidential."

"Goodwin said on the phone that you're blocked."

"We're stumped."

"But you still think it was premeditated murder?"

"Miss Denovo does, as Mr. Goodwin told you ten days ago. Do I? Yes, for reasons you might think deficient. But getting you here is not merely stumbling around in the dark. It isn't fatuous to assume that some recent event

duced the murder and that something connected with
that event, however remotely, was seen or heard by you.
In conversation with her, how did you address her? Mrs.
Denovo, or Elinor?"

"Elinor."

"Then I shall. How many others there called her Elinor?"

"Why . . . Let's see . . . three. No, four."

"Their names?"

"Now listen." Thorne flipped a hand. "That wouldn't
be just irrelevant trivialities, it would be drivel. It would
take three weeks, not just three days. Goodwin said someone at my place might be involved in it, and I told him
there wasn't the slightest chance. Simply impossible. Nobody there had any personal relations with her. Even I
didn't, actually. We often had meals together, lunch and
dinner and even breakfast sometimes, but only to talk
business." He turned to me. "I told you I soon saw she had
lines she didn't want crossed." Back to Wolfe: "I can give
you the names, sure, but I'm telling you, that will get
you nowhere."

"I would expect it to. On an excursion such as this
you get nowhere again and again. Very well, we'll try
another tack. When and where did you last see Elinor?"

"That Friday around noon at the studio. I was taking
a plane to the coast on business, to see a scriptwriter I
wanted."

"What studio?"

"Mine, of course."

"Did she speak of her plans for that evening?"

"Yes. *We* did. She was going to see a preview of a
movie for a look at an actor we thought we might want
to use."

"A preview where? At a theater?"

"No, a studio in the Bronx. That's why she took her
car. Of course I went over all this with the police. They
said she left the studio a little after ten that evening,
and I told them she probably went for a drive. She often
did. She said it relaxed her. I never saw her relaxed, not
really."

"Who went to the preview with her?"

"No one." Thorne emptied his glass and put it on th
stand, started a hand for the bottle, and pulled it bac
"That's marvelous cognac."

"Help yourself. I have nine bottles left. We'll start wit
that Friday and work back. How much were you wit
Elinor that morning?"

"Not much. There was a staff conference, but she ha
to leave it when someone came. Later I—"

"Who came?"

"A woman from an agency about a replacement the
client didn't like. Just routine. Agencies' clients never lik
anything. Later I dictated some notes to her. Of course
had my secretary and she had hers, but she still did shor
hand, and dictating to her made it different. It came o
better. She was a very remarkable woman. She had offe
of twice, three, or four times as much as she could mak
with me, agencies and public-relations people, but sh
turned them all down."

"Why?"

"I don't know. My guess was that they were mostly bi
outfits and she liked the complete freedom she had wit
me."

"What if I asked you to tell me everything you hear
her say that morning? Could you do it?"

"My God, no. Anyway it was just business. Ther
couldn't possibly have been anything with any hint o
what was going to happen to her that night. You know
I might be better at this if I knew why you think it wa
premeditated murder. Goodwin told me it was Amy's in
tution. Isn't a hit-and-run nearly always just a hit-and
run?"

"Yes. I would like to oblige you, Mr. Thorne, if onl
as a token of Miss Denovo's appreciation of your willing
ness to help, but I can't divulge information that th
police are reserving. Only five hours ago a police office
of high rank, discussing that hit-and-run with Mr. Good
win, said, 'He got a cigar out to light it while he wa
parked on Second Avenue waiting for her, and there sh
came.' If I were free to tell you more I would. Hel
yourself to brandy. If you please, Archie, beer?"

That was a fair example of how to lie while sticking t

e truth. It was perfectly true that he couldn't, or any-
ow shouldn't, divulge information that the police were
eserving. It was also true that a high-ranking police officer
ad said that to me. So a truth plus a truth equaled a
are-faced lie.

It was the only one he told during the four long hours
at Thorne sat in the red leather chair while downing
third of a bottle of marvelous cognac. I doubted if he
new how good it was; a man had once offered Wolfe fifty
ucks for a bottle of it.

The four hours took us an hour and a half past mid-
ight, into Friday morning, and the brandy took Thorne
nto a kind of talking trance that made him forget about
me, and also seemed to oil his memory, which was just
ack. He remembered Thursday a little better than Friday,
nd by the time they got back to Monday he was remem-
ering so much that I began to suspect him. He had
emarked at one point that he had done some script-
riting, so he had had practice making things up.

But he didn't make up *the* thing, the thing that hit. It
asn't a smack. I damned near let it slide by. I had been
tting there listening to irrelevant trivialities for more
han three hours; it was well past midnight, I had covered
t least a dozen yawns, and I had been drinking milk,
ot brandy. They had been on Monday for maybe twenty
ninutes, and had got to where Thorne and Elinor were
n their way out to have lunch with somebody, and Thorne
as telling how the receptionist had stopped Elinor to tell
er that Floyd Vance had been there again and she had
ad to threaten to call in a policeman if he didn't leave.
he receptionist said he might be out in the hall. Elinor
ad thanked her and they had left. Naturally Wolfe had
sked who Floyd Vance was, but Thorne knew nothing
bout him; he said probably some nut who wanted to
eddle an idea for a show that the networks would give
million for. They were a dime a dozen.

As I said, I nearly let it slide by. It hit me a little later
s I was telling my jaw and cheek muscles to get set to
ide another yawn, and I made a mistake. I forgot the
awn and my jaws opened wide for it. That led me into
second mistake, which often happens. Preferring not to
et Thorne know that he had told us a fact which might

be significant, I tried to go on as I had been for an hour,
looking more awake and alert than I was, and I overdid
it. If he had been awake and alert he would have noticed
it, but by that time his talking trance was in command
and it would have made no impression on him if I had
wiggled my ears.

But Wolfe noticed it, and that was what kept him from
going on and on and making a night of it unless Thorne
ran down. So it was only half past one and they had only
got to the middle of Monday afternoon when he looked at
the clock and said he was too tired to continue, and
Thorne must be too. Miss Denovo would deeply appreciate
Thorne's cooperation, and he and Mr. Goodwin would
see if they could find a hint in any of the items Thorne
had supplied. As Thorne used both hands on the chair
arm to get to his feet I was thinking that I would have to
steer him out and down the stoop steps, and possibly even
go and get the Heron to cart him home, but he did all
right. Going down the hall he put a hand to the wall once
to steady himself, and outside he stood and brought his
shoulders up and took a couple of deep breaths, but he
made it down to the sidewalk without any trouble. I stayed
to watch him for about thirty paces. Okay.

As I entered the office Wolfe growled at me, "You got
something. What?"

I went to my desk and sat. "Nothing would please me
more than to catch one you should have caught and
missed, but I can't claim it on this. I *think* we've got a
nibble. I don't know whether it's the father or the murderer, or possibly both, but I *think* it's a nibble. Last
Sunday afternoon at Miss Rowan's place in the country
three people came who had not been invited and weren't
expected. Two of them were friends of hers—well, ac-
quaintances; I had met them there before—who have a
place half an hour away. The third one was their weekend
house guest, a man named Floyd Vance. They said they
had mentioned to him that Archie Goodwin was often
at Lily Rowan's for weekends, and he had got them to
drive him over because he wanted to meet me. I gathered
from what he said that what he really wanted was to
meet you. He said he was a public-relations counselor. He

said that if anybody needed expert handling of his public image a private detective did, and he would like to create a presentation to propose to you. He also said that if we were working on a case and I would tell him about it, he could use that as a basis for the presentation. At that, naturally, I looked and listened, but decided he was just trying to find another sucker for his racket. I now sincerely hope I was wrong. Two comments. One, there are probably very few Floyd Vances around. Two, allowing for the twenty-three years, he fits Salvatore Manzoni's description just fine."

"I would like some beer," Wolfe said.

"You're already two bottles ahead and it's going on two o'clock."

"Satisfactory," he said, leaving it open whether he meant the beer or the nibble. He gripped the edge of the desk to push his chair back, rose, and headed for the hall. For a second I thought he was walking out, to go to bed with the nibble, but he turned left in the hall. He was going for beer. When he returned he had a bottle and a glass in one hand and a snifter in the other. He put the bottle and glass on his desk, got the cognac bottle from the stand and poured a couple of ounces in the snifter,

"You might easily have missed it," he said, and went around to his chair, opened the bottle, and poured.

I whirled the brandy around in the snifter and said, "I almost did. If it's only a coincidence I'm through with the detective business for good. We'll soon know, one way or another. The quickest and most obvious would be to have Salvatore Manzoni take a look at the public-relations Floyd Vance, but twenty-three years is a long time and it might not prove anything. Of course the receptionist at Thorne's could settle it that it was the public-relations Floyd Vance that she shooed out that May day, but that would only prove that it's a real nibble."

I put the snifter to my lips and tilted my head back enough to get a good gulp. Wolfe, having waited until the bead was down to precisely the right level, raised his glass.

"Fingerprints," I said.

"Yes," he said.

"We get his and give them to Cramer and they match or they don't."

"No." He licked foam from his lips. "If they matched we'd be in a fix. Mr. Cramer would have a murderer, but we would still need a father, and he would be locked up and inaccessible. You said he wanted to meet me."

"Yeah. If he's it, what he really wanted was to find out if we had got anywhere and if so how far. How he knew we were on it is a question, but we don't have to answer it. Sure, I could get him here, and then what? Do you think you could ask him anything that would help without giving him a guess that we're on him? I don't. There would be the same risk in seeing the receptionist at Thorne's. She might tell him."

He poured beer, leaned back and closed his eyes, and pushed his lips out. He pulled them in and pushed them out again. That was a new one; it had never happened before. The lip act, leaning back and closing his eyes and working his lips out and in, was routine; that meant he was working, working hard, and interruptions were not allowed. But that was the first time he had ever started it with beer just poured, and how would he handle it? How would he know when the bead was down to the right level with his eyes shut? By God, he did. When it was down to where it would just cover his lips as he drank, he opened his eyes, reached for the glass, drank, put the glass down, leaned back, closed his eyes, licked the foam off, and sent his lips out and in. I decided he must have practiced it when I wasn't around.

I usually time the lip act, since there's nothing else to do except try to guess what he'll come up with. That time it was three minutes and ten seconds. He opened his eyes, straightened up, and asked, "They're coming at nine o'clock?"

I said yes.

"I suppose a public-relations person has an address? An office?"

I got the Manhattan book and found the page. "Fourninety Lexington Avenue. Not the best. It should be Madison."

"Tell them to trace him back and cover nineteen forty-four thoroughly, but not to risk prompting him. That will be no problem with Saul and Fred, but with Orrie make it emphatic as usual."

"Right." I had emptied the snifter during the lip act, and as he pushed his chair back I went to pour another swallow. It might put me to sleep a few seconds quicker.

12

Not a fly. Flies don't buzz. Mosquito. No. Too loud. What the . . . Oh. House phone, for God's sake. I opened an eye, stretched an arm and got it, said, "Well?"

Fritz's voice said, "Good morning, Archie. He wants you."

I glared at the clock on the bedstand, realized that it actually said twenty-five minutes past eight, and swung my feet around. Figuring out whether I had failed to turn the alarm on, or it had tried to stir me and *it* had failed, would have to wait. I called for will power, gave it time to deliver, made it to my feet, concentrated on locating the door, and stepped.

The door of Wolfe's room, which is above the kitchen, at the rear of the house where he gets the sun in winter, stood open. When I entered, with my bare feet making no sound, he was seated at the table, with the *Times* propped on the rack, dropping a bit of toast into the sauce of eggs *au beurre noir*. When I cleared my throat he got the toast to and into his mouth before he turned his head.

"The time is out of joint," I said.

He frowned. "I don't talk in quotations, even Shakespeare, and neither do you."

"Miss Rowan does sometimes and she likes that one. As you see, I am no longer on daylight saving. Apparently you are." He was fully dressed: a nice clean yellow shirt with narrow maroon stripes, a maroon tie, and a brown summerweight self-striped suit. Up in the plant rooms he would shed the jacket and put on a smock.

He swallowed a bite of egg and said, "It's nearly nine o'clock."

"By daylight saving, yes, sir. I'll brief them while I'm eating breakfast."

"Only Saul. We won't risk it with Fred and Orrie. Tell them to be on call. You and Saul will decide on your approach and you may need them later. First, is he involved? If yes, merely as the murderer, with a motive that doesn't concern us, or also as the father? We can't waste our time and the client's money just on finding a culprit for Mr. Cramer." He dropped toast in the sauce.

"I'm waking up," I said. "Or I got ideas in my sleep. Last night I said we don't have to answer the question how he knew we were on it, but if he's the father it may be important. If he's the father there's some connection between him and Cyrus Jarrett, or why did Jarrett send the checks? And if Jarrett told him that Nero Wolfe is out to find the father, and if he is also the murderer, what about Miss Denovo? We might lose a client. I doubt if you want another casualty like Simon Jacobs on the record, and I certainly don't. I suggest that we'd better get her out of circulation."

He made a face. "Fritz."

That was what he calls flummery. It was true that when, for security reasons, it had been necessary to have a female guest sleeping and eating in the South Room, which is above Wolfe's, Fritz hadn't been able to hide how he felt about it, but Wolfe hadn't even tried to hide how *he* felt.

"I'm aware," I said, "that if we did it again Fritz might leave and you might too. I don't mean here. She spends most of her days at Miss Rowan's, and she could spend her nights there too until we get him or drop him. Miss Rowan has two spare rooms. I'll suggest it. Anything else?"

He said no and I went back up a flight to do in ten minutes what usually takes me thirty. By the time I got down to the kitchen, having stopped in the office to tell Fred and Orrie that Saul and I were going to pick up a trail and might need them later, my fog was starting to clear.

A detective is supposed to get onto things and people,

but I gave up long ago trying to get onto Fritz all the
way, so I didn't bother to try to guess how he had known
Fred and Orrie would be leaving and Saul would be staying. He knows Saul loves his eggs *au beurre noir,* and
there were two chairs and two places ready at my breakfast table. Saul went to the range to watch him baste,
and said he had tried it a hundred times but it never
tasted the same. As we ate I told Saul about Floyd Vance
and the various angles, and we took our second cups of
coffee to the office to consider ways and means. Wolfe had
said that the first question was, Is he involved? but Saul
agreed with me that it couldn't do any harm to regard
that as answered and proceed accordingly. He also agreed
that it would help if he had a look at him, and I got
at the phone and dialed the number of Nathaniel Parker,
the lawyer.

"Yes, Archie?" I like the way Parker says yes, Archie.
He knows that handling something for Wolfe can be
interesting but that it may be tough and ticklish, so the
yes, Archie is half glad and half sad.

I told him it was nothing much this time. "Just a little
chore. A man named Floyd Vance has an office at Fourninety Lexington Avenue. He's a counselor, but not at
law, at public relations, which as you know is a much
newer profession. The chore is to ring him and tell him
you have a client who is thinking of engaging his services,
and you would like to send a man to discuss it with him.
The name of the man is Saul Panzer, whose qualifications
you know about. He can go any time, the sooner the better.
I'm going out, but Saul will be here to take your call.
You have the name? Floyd Vance."

"I have it. What if he wants particulars?"

"You're not prepared to give him any."

"That's a good way to put it. I am certainly not prepared. Give the genius my regards."

He meant it, but he knew I knew exactly what he
would put in a long footnote. I dialed another familiar
number to make another request and then went up to
my room for a quick shave and change. The ten minutes
before breakfast hadn't been enough.

It was too hot to walk the more than two miles to
East Sixty-third Street, and anyway I had told Lily I

would be there by eleven-thirty. It was five minutes short of that when I pushed the button at the penthouse door and got a mild surprise when Mimi opened it. When I am expected at a certain hour it's nearly always Lily who comes, I think on account of some kind of a notion she has about a maid admitting a man who has a key. I have never tried to dope it. Other people's notions are none of my business unless they get in the way. Then I got a second mild surprise. I had told Lily on the phone that I wanted to see both her and Miss Denovo, but even so, why were they out on the terrace at that hour with a pitcher of iced tea when they should have been inside working? The penthouse was air-conditioned. Was Lily actually still . . . To hell with it. *I* was working. I moved another chair over, between them, sat, accepted an offer of tea with lime and mint, and said, "Don't mind my manners, I have a busy day ahead." I turned to Lily. "We're working on a problem for Miss Denovo. We've been on it—"

"Archie! No."

That was an example of a client's notion getting in the way. "I'm talking," I told her distinctly and returned to Lily. "It's very personal and she doesn't want anyone to know about it, not even you, and I'm proud and happy that she trusts me so much that she calls me Archie, so about her problem I'll only say that she is not responsible for it. Other people created it; she merely wants to solve it. She came to see Nero Wolfe two weeks ago today."

"Why do you—" Amy started, and stopped.

Lily was smiling at me. "Olé, Escamillo," she said, and put a kiss on a fingertip and flipped it to me.

"Last night," I told Amy, "there was a development. With Miss Rowan here I can't give you the details, and I wouldn't anyhow at this stage. But it is now more than a wild guess that your mother's death wasn't just an accidental hit-and-run, that it was deliberate murder, and if so it's possible that he has ideas about you. We don't know—"

"He? Who?"

"You have probably never heard the name we're interested in, and you won't hear it now. We don't know what motive he might have had for your mother, or if he has one for you, but once in a situation like this we made a bad mistake and once is enough." I turned to Lily. "Can she stay here? I mean *stay*. Not even go out in the hall. This terrace is okay; I doubt if he has a helicopter. Until we know more than we do now. Perhaps just a couple of days, but it could be a couple of weeks. You could get a lot of work done on the book."

"Why not?" Lily said. "Certainly."

Amy was squinting at me, squinting and frowning. "But you can't expect me . . . You can't just tell me . . ." She looked at Lily. "If you don't mind, Miss Rowan, I want to ask him something. I mean alone."

"I don't mind," Lily said, "but I know him better than you do. He's working. When he's playing he's wonderful —usually—but when he's working he's impossible. He said he wouldn't give you any details, but if you want to try I don't mind."

"I do," I told Amy. "I've got things to do, and anyway there's nothing I could or would tell you. This development may be a dud, and I've got to find out." I stood up. "You'll want to go to your apartment to bring things, but don't take all day." To Lily: "The standard rate for bodyguarding is six dollars an hour, but you shouldn't count the hours you're working on the book."

"May I take her to the country for the weekend?"

"No. It's barely possible we'll need her."

"You didn't drink the tea."

"And I'm thirsty." I picked up the glass, took a couple of swallows, kissed the top of her head, and went.

Before long the day will come, maybe in a year or two, possibly as many as five, when I won't be able to write any more of these reports for publication. There will be nothing to report because it will be so close to impossible to move around in the city of New York that doing detective work will be restricted to phone calls and distances you can walk, and what could anyone detect? It took a taxi forty-nine minutes that Friday to cover the four miles from East Sixty-third Street to the building where the New York Telephone Company keeps a file of old directories available for researchers, but once there, I needed only nine minutes to learn that Vance, Floyd, was listed in the 1944 Manhattan directory and his address had been Ten

East Thirty-ninth Street. It had to be a business address, because there were no residential buildings in that block. That was satisfactory on two counts: one, that he had been around in 1944, and two, that his office had been in walking distance of Tufitti's restaurant on East Forty-sixth Street for lunch or dinner. The next step, naturally, was to have a look at Ten East Thirty-ninth Street, but it had to wait because Saul was expected for lunch and a conference. When my taxi turned into Thirty-fifth Street from Ninth Avenue, Saul was just getting out of one double-parked in front of the old brownstone.

The next hour, at the lunch table, provided nourishment for both my stomach and brain. For the stomach, sweetbreads *amandine* in patty shells and cold green-corn pudding. For the brain, a debate on the question whether music, any music, has, or can have, any intellectual content. Wolfe said no and Saul said yes. I backed Saul because he weighs only about half as much as Wolfe, but I thought he made some very good points, which impressed me because one recent Thursday evening at his apartment he had been playing a piece by Debussy, I think it was, on the piano for Lon Cohen and me while we waited for the others to come for poker, and Lon had said something about the piece's intellectual force, and Saul had said no music could possibly have intellectual force. As the woman said to the parrot, it depends on who you're talking to.

In the office after lunch I told Wolfe what Saul and I had decided about the approach, including my phone calls to Nathaniel Parker and Lily, and then reported. "I did one thing," I said, "and learned one thing. I arranged for the client to stay put in Miss Rowan's penthouse until further notice, and I learned that in nineteen forty-four Floyd Vance had a telephone at an office at Ten East Thirty-ninth Street. There wasn't time to go and have a look, but I know that the wreckers haven't got to that block and the old buildings on the south side are still there. Unless Saul got something hotter we'll go and surround it."

Wolfe looked at Saul.

"Nothing even warm," Saul said. "It always helps to see a subject, but Archie had already seen him, so it's no news that he's a middle-aged slouch who may have been quite a fine figure twenty-three years ago. He has two little rooms, with him in one and a blonde with too much lipstick in the other, and when I asked about his past and present clients he either had very little to show or he wasn't showing me. Of course he wanted to know who Parker's client was, that was natural, but he pressed me on it more than he should have. I was getting so little that I almost made a mistake. I thought of asking him if he had ever had a television producer for a client, but of course I didn't. I was thinking on my way there that it might be possible to get something with a nice collection of his fingerprints on it, but he was right there with me in that little room. If he locks the door when he leaves that would be no problem. The lock's an ordinary Wingate. Archie or I could open it with our eyes shut."

Wolfe shook his head. "We have no use for fingerprints now. Possibly later."

"I know, but I thought it would be nice to have them. I mention it only because I can't match what Archie got —that nineteen forty-four address." Saul looked at me. "It's still August and the weekend starts in a couple of hours." He got up. "Let's go, you can plan it on the way."

For two able-bodied, quick-witted, well-trained men Saul and I accomplished a lot in the next two days. He got a haircut, which is quite a feat on a Saturday or Sunday in summer for a man who lives in midtown Manhattan. I detected it when I met him Monday morning. As for me, I frittered away $23.85 of the client's money on taxi fares and tips between ten a.m. and seven p.m. Saturday, which is also quite a feat. Just three doors away from Ten East Thirty-ninth Street was a lunchroom, Dwyer's, with a long fountain counter, and the manager told me it had been there for thirty years. He had himself been there nineteen years, and that meant only since 1948, but he knew the name of the man who had preceded him and he had an address in the Bronx where he had lived. The name was Herman Gottschalk, and I spent nine hours trying to track him down so I could show him photographs of seven young women.

That wasn't dumb; it was merely desperate. Of course the obvious place to look for someone to ask about the

tenants and frequenters of that building in 1944 was the
building itself, but Saul and I had pretty well covered that
Friday afternoon. There was no elevator man or other
service man who had been there more than four years
except the building superintendent. He had got the job
in 1961, soon after the building had been acquired by its
present owner, and he told Saul his predecessor had been
there only five years. He didn't even know the name of
the former owner or agent. He did know that none of
the present tenants had been there as long as twenty-three
years. At the Third Avenue office of the East and West
Realty Corporation, the current agent, the only personnel
on duty Saturday morning were a girl whose mother should
have made her wear teeth braces and an old man with
a glass eye who didn't even know the name of the pre-
vious owner or agent.

I accomplished something else on Sunday. I took Lily
Rowan and Amy Denovo to a double-header at Shea
Stadium, and got the client back to the penthouse safe and
sound.

Monday morning a sunburned woman at the East and
West Realty Corporation gave us the name of the pre-
vious agent, Kauffman Management Company, and at
their office on Forty-second Street we were lucky enough
to find a smart and active young man who believed in
giving service. He spent half an hour looking up old records. The man who had been the superintendent at Ten
East Thirty-ninth Street in 1944, named William Polk,
had died in 1962. There was no record of the names of
any of the service personnel, but there was a complete
list of the 1944 tenants—twenty-two of them, counting
Floyd Vance—and we copied it. The smart young man
said there was no one active in the Kauffman Management Company who had been there for twenty-three years.
Bernard Kauffman, who had founded it, was dead.

Saul and I each took half of the list of tenants and
went to work on them. I could make a full report on the
first four I tackled, but this is not a treatise on economics
or sociology. It was the fifth one that rang the gong, a
little before five o'clock in the afternoon—a woman named
Dorothy Sebor, fifty, gray-haired and blue-eyed and fully
as smart as the young man at the Kauffman Management

Company—who headed and probably owned the Sebor
Shopping Service in a tenth-floor suite at Rockefeller
Center. She was busy. The forty minutes I spent with her
wouldn't have been more than half that if the phone
hadn't interrupted several times, and I might have had a
problem getting to her if I hadn't sent in word that I
wanted to ask her something about Ten East Thirty-ninth
Street. When I entered her room she asked if I was the
Archie Goodwin who worked for Nero Wolfe, and when I
said yes she asked, "But what can I possibly tell you about
Ten East Thirty-ninth Street? I left eighteen years ago.
I loved that dump. Sit down."

I sat. "I don't know what you can tell me, Miss Sebor,
but I know what I want to ask. A job we're on goes back
pretty far and it's nineteen forty-four we're interested in.
Would you mind telling me what floor you were on?"

"No, why should I? The ninth. In the rear."

"We understand that another of the tenants was named
Floyd Vance. Did you know him?"

"I wouldn't say I *knew* him. I knew him by sight, he
was on the same floor, the ninth, down the hall toward the
front. We exchanged nods, remarks about the weather;
you know how it is."

My hand didn't want to go to my pocket. It had pulled
those damn pictures out too many times for too many people. But it obeyed orders and out came the seven photographs. "The quickest way," I said, "is for you to take a
look at these and tell me if you recognize anyone." As I
stretched an arm to hand them to her the phone rang, and
she put the pictures on the desk. When she finished telling
someone what to do and hung up she picked them up and
started looking. At the fourth one—I always had it in the
middle—she widened her eyes, looked at me, looked at
the photograph again, and said, "It's . . . not Vance . . .
Vaughn, that's it. Carlotta. Carlotta Vaughn." The blue
eyes aimed at me, a little narrowed. "I saw her name not
long ago, in an ad in two papers. The ad said something
about alias somebody."

"You knew her?"

"Yes. She worked for that Floyd Vance. Or with him,
I didn't know which."

I had two strong conflicting impulses simultaneously:

to give her a good hug and kiss her on both cheeks, and to pull her nose for not answering the ad a week ago. I put one of them into words. "Miss Sebor," I said, "you are the most beautiful woman I ever laid eyes on and if I knew what color you like I would buy you ten dozen roses. With our client's money, of course."

She smiled, more with her eyes than her mouth. "My shopping service hasn't worked much on florists, but it would be interesting to try. Apparently I've dealt you an ace."

"Four of them. You've answered a question that I was beginning to think would never be answered. If you will—"

"Is Carlotta Vaughn your client? No, of course not, not if you placed that ad. You're trying to find her?"

"No. She's dead. I'd like to tell you about it, but you're busy and it's a long story, and as our client says, it's *very* personal. If you'll answer a few more questions I'll be extremely grateful. Was it in—"

The phone. That time it took longer; she was telling someone what *not* to do. She finally finished it and returned to me. "I'll ask you a question, Mr. Goodwin. I liked Carlotta Vaughn, and she impressed me as a very competent young woman. I didn't see a lot of her—we had lunch together a few times—but I saw enough of her to be impressed. I was trying to get my business started and it was hard going, and I tried to persuade her to go in with me, as a partner, but she wouldn't. I liked her very much. You say she's dead. Would she approve of what you're doing?"

I lied. I could have dodged and wriggled, a lot of guff, that I hadn't known Carlotta Vaughn and therefore could only guess, and if and but and even so, but I preferred a straight lie. "Yes," I said, "she certainly would. It was a long time ago, but you may remember. When did you first see her?"

"That's easy. I'll never forget that first winter; I still have the scars. I started, rented that one room, in the fall of nineteen forty-three, and I first saw Carlotta the next spring—early spring, April, or it could have been March. I suppose the first time was in the hall or the elevator, I don't remember."

"Then she was there in the spring and summer of nineteen forty-four."

She nodded. "That's right, nineteen forty-four."

"Do you remember when you saw her last?"

"Not definitely, no. Not to name a date, but when I hadn't seen her for a while I asked Floyd Vance about her and he said . . ." She frowned and shook her head. "Something vague. She had gone somewhere or something."

"Was that in summer, or fall, or winter?"

"Not winter. By November my business was beginning to show some signs of life, and I wanted to tell Carlotta, but she wasn't there. It was probably in October."

"That would make it a total of six or seven months. You said you didn't know if she worked for Floyd Vance, or with him. But she was there every day, in his office?"

"I don't know about *every* day. But most of the time, yes, she was there. He was in public relations. I don't know if he still is, I know nothing about him. He left Number Ten—I think it was two years after Carlotta left."

"I have the impression that your liking for Carlotta didn't extend to him."

"It didn't. I didn't know him, really, and I didn't want to. He thought he was handsome and charming, and perhaps he was, but I thought he was—well, flashy. Not the kind of man I would work either for or with. And if you —good lord, is *he* your client?"

"He is not. I doubt if there are many men of any kind you would work for or with."

She smiled, more with her mouth than her eyes. "I've never tried and don't intend to. I wouldn't mind having a man of your kind working for me. How much does Nero Wolfe pay you?"

"Nothing. I work for love of the job. I meet interesting people like you. If I get fed up and quit I'll come and remind you. Speaking of quitting, do you suppose Carlotta quit Vance because her opinion of him was about the same as yours? She might have said—"

The phone again—an important customer, judging from the conversation—and then she made calls to two employees, giving one of them detailed instructions and the

her one hell. As she hung up she looked at her watch.
t's getting late," she said, "and I have a pile of work."

"So have I, thanks to you." I rose to my feet. "Do you
ppose your opinion of Vance rubbed off on Carlotta?"

"I doubt it. If it did she wouldn't have told me. She
as very . . . self-contained."

"Do you shake hands with men?"

She laughed—a good healthy laugh. "Occasionally. If
want them to do something."

"Then I qualify." I put a hand out. "You want me to
ave."

Her grip was firm and friendly. "If you get fed up,"
e said, "I could pay you fifteen thousand to start."

"I'll remember. What color roses do you like?"

"Green with black borders. If you sent me ten dozen
ses I'd sell them to some customer. I'm a businesswom-
1."

She certainly was.

13

When Wolfe came down from the plant rooms at si
o'clock, I was sprawled in my chair, no necktie, with m
shoes off and my feet up on one of the yellow chair
reading a magazine. As he crossed to his desk I gave hi
a lazy nod, yawned, and returned to the magazine. Th
sound came of his chair taking the seventh of a ton.
didn't see his glare because my back was turned, but
felt it. He demanded, "A stroke? The heat?"

I turned my head around casually. "No, sir, I'm fin
I'm just relaxing. Saul phoned a few minutes ago and
invited him to dinner. The job is finished. Floyd Vanc
is Miss Denovo's father. I was going to ring her and te
her, but maybe you'd rather tell her yourself."

"Pfui. Report."

I got my feet to the floor, no hurry, straightened u
and bent over to put my shoes on. When I am doing desl
work the door to the hall and most of the room are be
hind me, and on the wall back of my desk is a mirro
five feet wide and four feet high, for keeping an eye or
people. I used it to put my tie on, combed my hair wit
my fingers, swiveled, and said, "I don't suppose you'll eve
want the painful details of what led up to it, but if you do
I'll be glad to oblige. An hour and a half ago a woma
named Dorothy Sebor who runs, repeat runs, a shoppin
service in Rockefeller Center, said to me, 'But what can
possibly tell you about Ten East Thirty-ninth Street?
left there eighteen years ago. I loved that dump. Sit down.
If you don't mind I'll use my formula, not yours. I prefe
'I' and 'she' to 'Goodwin' and 'Sebor.'"

I gave it to him verbatim, with him, as always, leanin

116

back with his eyes closed. When I finished he sat for a full minute, no movement, and then moved only his lips to mutter, "Very satisfactory."

"It was about time," I said with feeling. "Questions."

His eyes opened. "Why roses?"

I nodded. "I expected that. It came out without thinking, probably because she had struck me as not the type for orchids. She could probably get a lot more for Nero Wolfe orchids than for run-of-the-nursery roses."

"We'll send her some sprays of Phalaenopsis Aphrodite. They have never been finer. Having had time to consider it, you regard the job as finished?"

"I was just smacking my lips after so many hungry days. One will get you fifty that Floyd Vance is the father, but I admit it wouldn't be enough for a jury. It might be enough for the client, but I also admit there are other angles."

"Specify them."

"Well. The angle most important to us is your honor. Four days ago I said to Cramer, 'I am authorized to give you Mr. Wolfe's word of honor that if we get anything you might be able to use we'll pass it on to you before we make any use of it ourselves.' I added, 'At least two minutes before,' but that didn't cancel the commitment. We now have these items: One: Carlotta Vaughn became pregnant in the summer of nineteen forty-four and almost certainly wasn't married. Two: she spent the entire summer of nineteen forty-four in close association with Floyd Vance. Three: on Monday, May twenty-second, nineteen sixty-seven, four days before Carlotta Vaughn, who was then Elinor Denovo, died, Floyd Vance tried to see her and was chased by the receptionist, and he had been trying to see her before. I'd hate to undertake to tell Cramer that those three items, taken together, are not something he might be able to use. Of course your honor is your lookout, but I mortgaged it."

He grunted. "My lookout and my responsibility. Go on."

"Then the angle that may interest me more than it does you. My honor isn't involved, but my feelings are, because I got my ass kicked twice by Cyrus M. Jarrett and I would like to return the compliment. What kind of a connection was there, and is there, between Jarrett and Vance that caused Jarrett to start sending checks to Carlotta Vaughn, alias Elinor Denovo, two weeks after her baby was born and to keep on sending them until her death? That could be another item that Cramer might be able to use, but that's not why *I* want to know. Also, of course, Miss Denovo would like to know. I believe in satisfying the client. I also believe in satisfying me. All right, I withdraw my brag; the job is *not* finished. It's your move."

I expected him to start the lip act, but he merely cocked his head. "The point," he said, "is that we don't know which of two alternative situations faces us. If he is the father but not a murderer, establishing it will be difficult if not impossible. He did that many years ago. But if he is also a murderer the situation is much simpler; he did that only three months ago. We'll resolve that and then decide how to proceed. Can you get him here this evening?"

"For what? Do I ask him if he still wants to meet you?"

"That would do to start. If he says no, tell him I want to meet him. Tell him I want to ask him why he didn't reply to the advertisement requesting information about Carlotta Vaughn, alias Elinor Denovo."

I had noted the listing of Vance's home phone, but got the directory to check on the number, and found that my memory had it right. It was a quarter to seven when I dialed, and if he ate out I would probably get no answer. But after two rings I got a hello.

"Mr. Floyd Vance, please?"

"I'm Floyd Vance."

"I'm Archie Goodwin. I work for Nero Wolfe. You may remember that we met at Lily Rowan's place, and you—"

"I remember."

"And you said you would like to meet Nero Wolfe to make a proposal. I reminded Mr. Wolfe of that just now when we were discussing something, and he decided he would also like to meet you. Could you come this evening, say at nine o'clock?"

Silence. Five seconds. "This is short notice."

"I know. It's not as urgent as a five-alarm fire, but if it's not too inconvenient . . . the address is—"

"I know the address." Silence. "You say nine o'clock?"

"Right. Or later if that would suit you better."

"Don't be so goddam polite. I'll be there around nine."

As I hung up, the doorbell rang, and I went, expecting Saul, and it was. I opened the door only a couple of inches and said through the crack, "You may not want to come in. No champagne. There are angles."

It was my fault. When Saul had phoned I had just got home, so pleased with myself and wanting to spread joy around that I had not only invited him to dinner but had also told him I would have a bottle of Dom Pérignon ready to open. Then the angles had made it obvious that putting champagne in the refrigerator would be premature and I hadn't gone to the kitchen. Not that Saul needed any explanations or apologies; that long dry spell had got on his nerves too.

Anyway, along with the clams and broiled turtle steaks he drank more than half of a bottle of Montrachet, so all he missed was bubbles.

With coffee, in the office after dinner, we settled the program. When Vance arrived Saul would go to the front room, and as soon as the guest was in the office and seated he would leave, to go to 490 Lexington Avenue and collect likely objects for fingerprints. Since he had seen the lock he knew which keys to take from the assortments in the cabinet, and after he made his selections he helped me prepare the props in the office. We did a thorough wiping job on twelve objects: the stand by the red leather chair, two ash trays—one on the stand and one on the corner of Wolfe's desk—two photographs of Elinor Denovo in a drawer of Wolfe's desk, four glasses of different kinds, since we didn't know what he would drink, two books of matches—one on the stand and one on Wolfe's desk—and every inch of the red leather chair. Now and then I took a second for a glance at Wolfe, for comic relief. He sat with his fingers laced at the summit of his center mound, scowling at us. He knew darned well that what we were doing was a lot more important than anything he could possibly be thinking, and it hurt. He would have loved to take the position, and hold it, that he could solve any problem on earth or in outer space by leaning back and closing his eyes and working his lips. The trouble was that the little chores Saul and I did for

him were nearly always done somewhere else, but that
time it was going on right there in his office, before his
eyes. I was surprised that he didn't get up and go to the
kitchen.

Amy's father rang the doorbell at ten after nine. As I
went to admit him Saul headed for the connecting door to
the front room, and as I took him to the office and to the
red leather chair I did something that I had done many
times although I had learned long ago that it was absolutely useless. For a spectator in a courtroom to try to decide from a man's looks if he's guilty or not is natural and
he has to pass the time somehow, but for a working detective it's pure crap. So I did it again. I looked at Vance's
puffed eyes, flabby cheeks, thin hair, saggy shoulders,
down to his brown shoes that needed a shine, actually
hoping to get a slant on the question, Did he kill Elinor
Denovo? Nuts.

By the time I got to nuts Wolfe was saying, ". . . not
that I scorn all trite expressions; some of the finest words
and phrases in the language were once vulgarisms and
are well worn. But a faddish cliché like 'image' as now
abused is an abomination. You told Mr. Goodwin that
my 'public image' needs expert handling and you would
like to meet me. If you have some proposal to make I'll
listen as a matter of courtesy, but don't call my repute
my image."

"To hell with your courtesy. Shove it." Vance's voice
was not as I remembered it. I had thought he was a
fairly smooth talker that Sunday, but now the words came
out blurry. He went on, "I've learned something about you
since I talked with Goodwin. You don't give a damn about
your public image. Did you get me here just to tell me
you don't like clichés? Do I go home now?"

Wolfe nodded. "That's your question, why I got you
here. My question is, Why did you come? I doubt if
either of us expects a candid answer. In fact, Mr. Vance,
I'm in some confusion about my objective. One possibility is that I would like to know why you prevailed on
your friends to drive you to Miss Rowan's so you could
meet Mr. Goodwin. Another possibility is that I would
like to know why you made several attempts to see Mrs.
Elinor Denovo last May. Still another is that I want to

ask you about your association with Miss Carlotta
Vaughn in the summer of nineteen forty-four. And again,
another is that I wondered why you didn't reply to an
advertisement which appeared—"

"Jesus. Give me a pad and pencil. I'll have to make
notes."

We hadn't wiped a pad. You can't think of everything.
I got one from a drawer, and a pencil, and went with
them, and he took them, probably because he was un-
certain what to do with his tongue and so was glad to
have something to do with his hands.

"As you see," Wolfe said, "I have—since you fancy
clichés—an embarrassment of riches." His head tilted; I
hadn't sat. "Beer, please, Archie?"

"Yes, sir." I took a step and stopped. "Something wet,
Mr. Vance?"

He shook his head and said emphatically, "No." I
started out, foiled because a glass or bottle is a best bet,
and as I neared the door his voice stopped me. "What
the hell. Scotch and water. And ice."

Fritz, having been told that he wouldn't be needed,
had gone out. In the kitchen I put Wolfe's beer and glass
on a tray, and on another tray a wiped glass, a bowl which
I wiped before putting icecubes in it, a pitcher which I
wiped before putting water in it, and a bottle of Johnnie
Walker Black which I also wiped. That took a while and
made me miss something. When I got to the office with
the trays Vance had used his hands some more and had a
cigar lit, so I didn't know if he carried them loose or in a
case, or if he had used the matches on the stand. The
cigar was a long panatela, nothing like a Gold Label
Bonita, but that didn't bother me; if he had left that case
in the hit-and-run car it would have been common prudence to switch. After serving the trays I went back to
the kitchen for a glass of milk and when I returned to the
office Vance had his glass in his hand and Wolfe was
talking.

". . . for I have no intention or desire to make any
demand or indictment, and I don't think my client has
either. I want only what I have been hired to get, information. I can't name my client, but if my questions reveal
her identity to you, that in itself would answer my basic

question. The advertisement plainly implied that the woman once known as Carlotta Vaughn was later known as Elinor Denevo, but if you prefer to tell me nothing about Elinor Denovo we'll restrict it to Carlotta Vaughn. By the way . . ."

He opened a drawer and took out the two photographs. I had cautioned him not to handle them in a way that would make it obvious that he was taking care not to leave prints—the Police Department files already had samples of his—and he did all right, perfectly normal as he handed them to me and I passed them on to Vance.

"She was Elinor Denovo when those were taken," Wolfe said, "but had been Carlotta Vaughn only a year or two previously, so you should recognize her."

Vance handled them normally too. He had put his glass down, and with one in each hand he gave them a look, first the three-quarters face and then the profile. He looked at Wolfe. "So what? Sure I recognize her." He put the photographs on the stand. "I'm not denying that I once knew a woman named Carlotta Vaughn." He picked up his glass and drank.

"When and where did you first meet her?"

"In the spring of nineteen forty-four." He was no longer blurring his words; apparently a few swallows of Scotch with very little water had helped. "I think it was late March. My God, it was twenty-three years ago."

"Where?" Wolfe had opened his bottle but hadn't poured.

"I don't remember. I suppose some party. I was under thirty and I got around."

"And you hired her?"

"Well . . . yes."

"You paid her a salary?"

Vance took a swallow. "Look," he said, "I'm not going to toot my horn. As I said, I was under thirty, and girls were no problem. They seemed to like my style. This Carlotta Vaughn got it hard. I wasn't setting any rivers on fire in my business and she knew it—what the hell, everybody knew it—and she wanted to help, and she was smart. So I let her help. No, I didn't pay her."

"How long did she continue to help?"

"Oh, all summer. Into fall. Six months, perhaps seven."

"Why did she stop?"

"I didn't ask her. She just stopped."

"I think you can improve on that, Mr. Vance. Didn't she stop because she was pregnant?"

Vance tapped ashes from the cigar into the ash tray, put it between his lips and found it was out, took the book of matches from the stand and lit it, and blew smoke. He looked at Wolfe, opened his mouth and shut it, reached for the bottle and poured Scotch, picked up the glass, took a swig, and looked at Wolfe again.

"Yes," he said. "She was storked. So she said. It didn't show."

"So you had impregnated her."

"The hell I had."

"Certainly."

"For God's sake. She was a nymph. She was a goddam tart. She didn't know herself who knocked her up. She admitted it. To me."

That showed, if we had needed showing, how impossible it would be to tag him as the father. There were three people—Raymond Thorne, Bertram McCray, and Dorothy Sebor—who would contradict him on Carlotta Vaughn's morals and habits, and we could probably get more, but that would just be a squabble. However, he had a wide-open flank. What would he or could he say to the question, why did Cyrus M. Jarrett send her a thousand dollars a month as long as she lived? I decided he could say, and almost certainly would say, search me. Wolfe was probably making the same decision. He had poured beer and was watching the bead go down; of course he could merely have been thinking that Vance had used a cliché that was still a vulgarism. He turned his head to me and asked, "Is there any point in persisting?"

Meaning, have we got enough fingerprints?

"No," I said. Meaning yes.

He looked at his glass. The foam was down to the right level, exactly. He pushed his chair back, rose, and walked out. As he disappeared in the hall I told myself, for the twentieth time, that the furniture should be rearranged, so he wouldn't have to detour around the red leather chair when there was someone in it. An exit like that should be a beeline so you can stride.

I told Vance, "Serves you right. You used another cliché."

"Isn't he coming back?"

"Sure, after you've gone."

"What the hell, you could have asked me on the phone, any time, if I knocked her up and I would have told you."

"Yeah, I tried to tell him that. He thought that question was too personal for the phone. Also he likes to do things the hard way, and he likes to hear himself talk."

He looked at his glass, saw that there was a couple of fingers in it, picked it up, and drained it. "I thought he was going to . . ." He let it hang, and started over. "He said he would like to know why I tried to see that Elinor Denovo. What the hell, I wanted that account, Raymond Thorne Productions. I didn't know she was Carlotta Vaughn. The first I heard of that was that ad in the paper."

"You don't hear an ad in the paper. You hear an ad on the radio. You *see* an ad in the paper. On television you both hear it *and* see it. It's getting very complicated, and before we know it we'll—"

"Balls. I've heard enough of *you*. You're a pair of goddam loudmouths." It wasn't as easy as falling off a log to rise from that chair, and four of his fingertips pressed against the leather arm as he used leverage. When he was erect he told me to go do something, still another vulgar cliché, and I moved to get to the hall ahead of him; he might turn left instead of right, and Wolfe was in the kitchen. I didn't go to the front to open the door for him. Not because he was a liar; it just didn't seem to be called for.

When the door had shut behind him, with a bang, I went and opened the kitchen door enough to call through, "Company's gone!" and then to the stairs down to the basement storeroom for empty cartons and tissue paper and twine.

When I got back up to the office, loaded, Wolfe was standing at the end of his desk, frowning around at everything in sight. I put the cartons down on the couch and the paper and twine on my desk, and said, "I wouldn't trade images with that specimen, public or private. I

ave never felt so sorry for a client. If she had known
what she was going to get for her twenty grand . . ."

He growled. "How long will that cigar smoke last?"

"The air conditioner will do it in about an hour." I
was gently wrapping in tissue paper the glass that had
held Scotch. "I need your help on a decision. The bottle
is more than half full of Johnnie Walker Black. About
six dollars' worth. Do we donate it to Cramer or do I
empty it?"

"Empty it in the sink. It's contaminated. Confound this
smell. I'm going upstairs, but there's a letter to write.
Your notebook."

I went and sat, and for the first time in I don't know
how long he dictated a letter standing.

*"Dear Mr. Cramer: Five days ago you told Mr. Good-
win you had in your possession a leather cigar case from
which you had taken nine fingerprints. Period. The cartons
he will deliver to you with this letter contain an assortment
of objects, comma, some of which may have on them
fingerprints which may possibly match those you secured
from the cigar case. Period. This is merely a conjecture,
comma, and I shall be obliged if you will tell me whether
it is valid. Sincerely yours.* Fritz can bring it up with my
breakfast for my signature. By the time you and Saul
finish here I may be asleep."

He pinched his nose, told me good night, and headed
for the door.

14

When I arrived at the headquarters of Homicide South on West Twentieth Street at a quarter to nine Tuesday morning, I was on the fence. I wanted the cartons to get to Cramer as soon as possible, but if he was there I didn't want to deliver them to him myself, because as soon as he read the letter I would be stuck. He would hold me until the prints had been lifted and compared, and if they matched I would be held tighter and longer. So I was just as well pleased that he hadn't come yet. Neither had Purley Stebbins, but I got a sergeant I knew named Berman. When he saw the six cartons, one big enough to hold a wastebasket, which was one of the items Saul had brought from 490 Lexington Avenue, he said he hoped it wasn't all bombs and I said no, only one was, and the trick was to guess which. He put the letter in his pocket and promised to give it to Cramer as soon as he came.

It would be instructive to report how Saul got a big wastebasket out of that office building at ten o'clock at night, but it would take a page.

Home again, having had only orange juice before leaving, I ate breakfast, tried to find something in the *Times* that deserved attention, and expected. The trouble with expecting is that you always jump the gun. It could take anywhere from one to eight hours for them to get the prints lifted and compared, but as I went to the office to dust and tear pages from desk calendars and put fresh water in the vase on Wolfe's desk and open the mail, I was expecting the phone to ring any minute. You simply can't help it, especially when you have no good reason to bet a dime either way on what you're expecting. If the

126

fingerprints didn't match we were left with a Grade A
mess and no way on earth of making a neat package of it
to deliver to the client; if they did match we could take
our pick of three or four different ways to play it and they
all looked good. So I expected, and although I opened the
mail and gave it a look before putting it under the chunk
of jade on Wolfe's desk, I had no clear idea what was in
it. One thing, not in the mail, did get some real attention.
Saul and I had decided that we almost certainly had
enough without lifting the prints from the red leather chair.
We had got bed sheets from the closet and draped them
over it, and there it was, and it looked pretty silly. I
removed the sheets, folded them, and put them back in
the closet. What the hell, as Amy's father would say, I
was there on guard. Returning to the office, I looked at
my watch for about the tenth time since breakfast, saw
that it was 10:38, and decided it was time to consider it
calmly and realistically. To begin with, if the prints didn't
match there was nothing to expect. Some detective second grade would phone in a day or two to tell me to come
and get the junk I had left there. If they did match the
best guess was that Lieutenant Rowcliff or Sergeant Stebbins would phone around two or three o'clock and tell
me they wanted me there quick. Or possibly—

The doorbell rang and I went to the hall and saw
Cramer and Stebbins on the stoop.

Ordinarily the sight of a pair of cops wanting in doesn't
scatter my wits, but as I started for the front I had room
in my skull for only one item: the beautiful fact that the
prints had matched and Floyd Vance had murdered
Elinor Denovo. I should have realized that their coming
twenty minutes before eleven o'clock, when they knew
Wolfe wouldn't be available, showed that it would take
handling. Before I opened up I should have put the chain
bolt on, holding the door to a two-inch crack, since it would
have taken a warrant to open it legally and they wouldn't
have one, and we could discuss the situation. But I was
so glad to see them that I swung the door wide, and I was
probably showing my teeth in a big grin of welcome. If
so, it soon went. They came in fast, Stebbins' shoulder
jostling me as he passed, headed for the rear, and started
up the stairs.

A cop inside the house is a very different problem from
one outside. Once he's inside legally, and I had opened
the door, about all you can do is sit down and write a
letter to the Supreme Court. Even if I could beat them
to the plant rooms, and I couldn't, since the elevator was
up there, what good would it do? I went to the kitchen to
tell Fritz what had happened and that I was going up to
join the party, and then took my time mounting the three
flights.

To go through those three rooms, the cool, the moder-
ate, and the warm, down the aisles between the benches,
without being stopped by a color or a shape that you
didn't know existed, your mind must be fully occupied
with something else. That time mine was. In the middle
room I could already hear a voice, and when I opened
the door to the warm room I could name it. Cramer. I
walked the aisle and opened the door to the potting room,
and there they were. Wolfe, in a yellow smock, was on
his stool at the big bench. Theodore was standing over
by the pot racks. Stebbins was off to the right. Cramer, in
the center of the room, had his felt hat off and in his
hand, I don't know why. Facing Wolfe, he was telling
him, louder than necessary, ". . . and hold you as material
witnesses until we get warrants and then, by God, you
go to a cell. All right, talk or move."

Wolfe stayed on the stool. His eyes came to me. "Any
complaint, Archie?"

"Only their bad manners. Next time they'll talk through
a crack."

His eyes moved. "Mr. Cramer. As I said, I will not
talk business in this room. Not a word. If you'll wait in
my office I'll be down at eleven o'clock. If you put hands
on me, and Mr. Goodwin, and take us elsewhere, we'll
stand mute and communicate with our lawyer. When he
comes we'll confer with him privately, and the afternoon
paper, the *Gazette,* and tomorrow morning's papers, will
publish the news that Nero Wolfe and Archie Goodwin
have discovered the identity of the murderer of Elinor
Denovo and have delivered satisfactory evidence to the
police. Also, that in recognition of that public service they
have been arrested and are behind bars, and their lawyer
is arranging to secure their release on bail. Archie, here

please. This Miltonia charlesworthi germination card has conflicting entries. We'll have to check it."

I went and took the card and scowled at it.

Cramer was in a box. My taking him the contents of those cartons and the letter, if the prints matched, certainly made us material witnesses, but if he herded us downtown and we performed as programmed by Wolfe, and we would, he would have to plug his ears for the horse laughs. If he and Stebbins waited there to go down to the office with us there was nowhere to sit, and standing around waiting may be all right for a sergeant but not for an inspector.

Stebbins muttered, apparently to himself, "God, I'd love to knock him off that stool." He looked at Cramer. "We take 'em down and lock 'em up and kick 'em out before the lawyer comes."

Actually Cramer is not a fool, not at all. Stebbins must have sold him the bright idea of coming before eleven and invading the plant rooms. He jerked his head and a hand toward the door, an order, and the sergeant obeyed. He stepped to the door and opened it, and when Cramer was through he followed him, leaving the door wide open. Theodore went and shut it, and Wolfe looked at the electric clock which controlled the temperature and some of the ventilation. It was six minutes to eleven.

I asked, "Is this card really off?"

"No. Stay here." He turned to Theodore. "Those Odontoglossum pyramus aren't ready for sevens. Put them in sixes. Do you agree?"

"No," Theodore said. "A little extra room won't hurt them any."

I didn't listen to that argument, which took ten minutes; I was concentrating on what Cramer and Stebbins would find when they went through our desks, and congratulating myself for having undraped the red leather chair. I had to stay, of course, not only because Wolfe had told me to; if I had followed them down they would have started in on me and I might overdo it, the way I felt.

They would probably be expecting us to come down together in the elevator, so when Wolfe left the stool and unbuttoned the smock I said I would take the stairs and went. Since all three flights are carpeted, noise was no problem, and they didn't even know I was there, in the office doorway, until I spoke. Stebbins was seated at my desk, with two drawers open, and Cramer was over by the cabinets but with none of them open because they had locks.

I said, "I hadn't opened the safe yet. Sorry."

Cramer about-faced and narrowed his eyes at me. Stebbins merely took more papers from a drawer and started leafing through them. A cop inside the house. The sound came of the elevator descending, and it stopped, and as Wolfe came I stepped into the office. He entered, halted, shot a glance at Cramer, glared at Stebbins, who went right on with papers, and said, "Get Mr. Parker. I'll take it in the kitchen."

"What did you expect?" Cramer demanded. "Knock it off, Purley. Goodwin wants his chair. Come on, move!"

Stebbins tossed papers on my desk, a mess, got to his feet in no hurry, and went to get one of the yellow chairs. He likes to be with his back to a wall. By the time he had the chair where he wanted it Cramer was in the red leather chair and Wolfe, at his desk, had a drawer open to see if it was in order. He made a face and turned to Cramer. "The briefer we make this the better. You want to know who made those fingerprints."

"You're damned right I do. And I want—"

"I know what you want, but something I want comes first. I will not have that man"—he aimed a straight finger at Stebbins—"in my house. Ransacking my office? Pfui. I would like to exclude you too, but someone even less tolerable would probably replace you. Archie. On a letterhead, Mr. Vance's name and both addresses and telephone numbers. One carbon."

It took longer than usual to get paper and carbon in the typewriter on account of the mess Stebbins had made. As I typed Cramer said something, saw that Wolfe wasn't listening and didn't intend to, and shut his trap. As I rolled the paper out Wolfe said, "One to each," and I went and handed Cramer the original and Stebbins the carbon, and Wolfe told Cramer, "Get him out of here."

You have to admit that he knows when he can get away with what. In any ordinary circumstances he wouldn't have tried telling Cramer to get Stebbins out of there, but I had just given him the name and address of a man who had left his cigar case in a hit-and-run car.

Cramer said to Wolfe, "Floyd Vance. Was it his prints on that stuff you sent me?"

Wolfe said, "Yes. He made most of them last evening, in my presence, and Mr. Goodwin's, sitting in that chair."

Cramer turned to Stebbins and said, "Get him and take him in."

Stebbins got up and went.

So that man was out of there. As he turned into the hall Wolfe said, "You have been scampering around on a hot day and would presumably like something to drink, but you have forfeited your right to civilities. We've given you the name of a man you've been seeking for more than three months. What else do you want?"

The air conditioning had dried the sweat on Cramer's forehead and taken some of the red from his face. "I want plenty," he said. "I want one good reason why you and Goodwin shouldn't be charged with withholding information of a crime and obstructing justice. I want to know how long you have known that this Floyd Vance was the driver of that hit-and-run car, and how you spotted him. I want to know if he's the father you said you were looking for, and if so, and Elinor Denovo was the mother, I want to know why he killed her."

"That will take a lot of talking, Mr. Cramer."

"It sure will. Even for you. Go right ahead."

Wolfe adjusted his bulk in the chair. "First, withholding information. Last Thursday Mr. Goodwin gave you our word that if we got anything you might be able to use we would pass it on to you before we made any use of it ourselves. We got those fingerprints late last evening and delivered them to you early this morning, and we have made no use of them and don't intend to. I have no other information that you might be able to use, in my judgment."

"To hell with your judgment. If you think you can decide—"

"If you *please*. You told me to talk. As I told you, my client was, and is, a young woman who hired me to find her father. We found one likely prospect but investigation conclusively eliminated him. We found another, but he too was eliminated. I was inclined to return the retainer and withdraw, and persisted only because I am what I call tenacious and Mr. Goodwin calls pigheaded. Do you recognize the name Raymond Thorne?"

"Raymond Thorne? No."

"Doubtless some of your staff would. Elinor Denovo spent most of her adult life working for him. Raymond Thorne Productions. Television. He came at my request last Thursday evening and answered questions for more than four hours, and one of the many things I learned was that a man named Floyd Vance had tried several times last May to see Elinor Denovo, and she had refused to see him. His last attempt to see her was on the twenty-second of May, only four days before she died. If you had questioned the receptionist at Raymond Thorne Productions with sufficient perseverance you might have solved that case long ago. We made long and laborious inquiries about Floyd Vance and discovered that he had known Elinor Denovo in nineteen forty-four, when she was Carlotta Vaughn, and had seen her frequently for several months. It was possible that he was the father I was trying to find, and we tackled him. He is a self-styled public-relations counselor—one of the various modern activities that are an insult to the dignity of man. Mr. Goodwin got him here last evening. Preparations had been made. His attempts to see Elinor Denovo shortly before her death prompted the surmise that he had killed her, and, knowing that you had fingerprints, Mr. Goodwin and Mr. Panzer made proper arrangements. That was fortunate, but not for me, for you. Without that you would probably never have found him. And here you come—"

"I'm supposed to pin a medal on you?"

"I don't like medals. The fingerprints didn't help me any. He denied that he had fathered a child by Carlotta Vaughn. He could have been lying, certainly, but I was helpless. And am. Even if he is the man I'm looking for there is no conceivable way to establish it. Can you suggest one?"

"I handle homicides, not paternity suits."

"So you do. Now, with those fingerprints, you can handle this one. You said you want to know why he killed

her. So do I. I haven't the slightest notion. I have told
you everything I know about him. I have seen him only
once, here last evening, and I asked him no questions
pertaining to Elinor Denovo's death. I asked him nothing
about his attempts to see her in May. Now, of course, you
will, because you need a motive, and it's possible that
you will uncover one that will have a bearing on *my*
problem. If you do, and if you can share it with me
without hazard to your case, I'll try to erase from memory
this morning's outrageous performance. It won't be easy
—especially the sight of that creature at Mr. Goodwin's
desk, deranging his and my belongings, while you stood
and applauded."

"I did *not* applaud. Your usual exaggeration."

"You permitted."

"Oh, skip it. A cop gets habits like everybody else. He
was looking for information, not evidence. Even if he
had found Goodwin's signed confession that he had
killed Elinor Denovo it wouldn't have been admissible
evidence; ask the Supreme Court." Cramer looked at his
watch and then at me. "How long has he been gone?"

"Maybe fifteen minutes," I told him. "When you get
up don't put your hand on the right chair arm. It has
four Floyd Vance prints on it."

"Thanks for telling me." He put both palms on the
right chair arm and twisted around as he got to his feet.
He faced Wolfe. "I want to be there when he brings him
in. I admit you sound good, but you nearly always do
sound good. I'm buying nothing, at least not until I see
this Floyd Vance. If it goes one way you may hear from
me, and if it goes another way you *will* hear from me.
Have I ever thanked you for anything?"

"No."

"And I'm not thanking you now. Not yet." He turned
and went. I stayed put.

Wolfe opened his desk drawer to take another look, and
I attacked the mess Stebbins had made. Vandalism. There
was no danger that he had taken anything important
because no classified items were ever left in an unlocked
drawer, and after getting things in order and back where
they belonged I decided that he had taken nothing, except possibly a few of my calling cards. That suggested

the question, if it's illegal for a private detective to impersonate a cop why isn't it illegal for a cop to impersonate a private detective? I would ask Wolfe. He had shut the drawer and was leaning back, looking thoughtful but not concentrated. When I turned to him he nodded and said, "Phalaenopsis Aphrodite sanderiana."

I said, "If this is a quiz: rose, brown, purple, and yellow."

"We'll send some to that Dorothy Sebor, and I'll go up and get them now. I intended to bring them down but those intruders came. Also I brought none for my desk." He pushed his chair back.

"Instructions?"

"No. There is nothing you can do."

"Saul is standing by. So are Fred and Orrie."

"Release them. There is nothing. Our next step is obvious, but it must wait until Mr. Cramer learns his motive. *If* he learns his motive. He should, with a thousand trained men."

After the sound came of the elevator starting up I sat and looked it over from every angle. It was nice to know the next step was obvious, but it would have been even nicer to know what it was.

15

I didn't know then, and I still don't, exactly how long it took the city employees to find out why Floyd Vance killed Elinor Denovo. I mean really wrap it up. All I know is that Cramer's phone call didn't come until 6:38 p.m. Thursday, just in time to make me late at the poker party again. And I still didn't know what the obvious step was. One of the eighty-seven facts about Wolfe that I would change if I knew how is that he doesn't believe in talking merely to satisfy anyone's curiosity, even mine. I admit that in this case there might have been other factors —for instance, he might have wanted to see if I would dope it out for myself and make some suggestions. You probably have, but maybe you wouldn't if you had been in my shoes, waiting for a development which depended entirely on other people, and you didn't know what they were doing and not doing.

I did do one thing. When I learned from the noon news broadcast on Wednesday that Floyd Vance was being held without bail, and rang Lon Cohen to check it, I phoned Lily Rowan to say I wanted to see the client and was invited to lunch; and after we had finished the lobster salad and cantaloupe mousse and had gone out to the terrace, I told Amy that there was no more danger of her being a special target and if she went out for a walk her chances of getting back in one piece were as good as anybody else's. Naturally she wanted to know what had happened, and Lily did too, and I think that was the first and only time that Lily suspected me of putting on an act in connection with my work. She remembered that she had a date, some kind of a committee meeting, which I doubted, and left me there with Amy. I admit she thought she was being considerate, but it was no favor to me. I had been stalling Amy for two weeks and she wanted to know, and I couldn't blame her. Usually you can tell a client *something,* but I had already told her that her mother's name was Carlotta Vaughn, and there was absolutely nothing that I was ready to add. When I left I wasn't at all sure that I was still the one man in the world she could trust.

Of course I read every word in the Wednesday and Thursday papers about the hit-and-run driver the police had nabbed after three months, but learned nothing about motive. I got the impression that the fingerprints which had identified him had been secured by extremely competent detective work by the Homicide Bureau, but there were no published details about it. There was no mention of Nero Wolfe or Archie Goodwin. There was a lot of new information, new to me, about Floyd Vance, and one item cleared up a point that I had wondered about. In 1944 he had been in his late twenties and single, and why hadn't he been sent, either to Europe or to Asia, to help several million of his fellow citizens do some expert handling of the public image of the United States of America? According to Wednesday's *Gazette* and *News,* and Thursday's *Times,* he had been excused because he had some kind of a trick knee. Other items, though they cleared up nothing, told me more about him—for instance, that he had always been a tadpole in a big frog pond as a public-relations counselor. Evidently he had had very little effect on the dignity of man, either way.

When the phone rang at 6:38 p.m. Thursday, I was at my desk working on germination records and Wolfe was at his with a book he had just started on, an advance copy of *The Future of Germany,* by Karl Jaspers. I reached for the receiver.

"Nero Wolfe's office, Archie—"

"I want Wolfe, Goodwin. Cramer."

"Greetings." Without bothering to cover the transmitter, I turned my head and said, "Cramer," perhaps a little louder than usual, and Wolfe reached for his phone, perhaps a little faster than usual. I kept mine.

"Yes, Mr. Cramer?"

"About Floyd Vance. You read the papers."

"Yes."

"We're going for first-degree and we expect it to stick. We've followed the new rules and we don't even ask him if he's thirsty unless his lawyer's present. I'm willing to give you some information we haven't released if you give me your word that you'll keep it in confidence."

"That's rather difficult. Information that I can't use won't help."

"I doubt if you can use it. If you can use it without divulging it, okay."

"Very well. You have my word."

"For what you want, it's negative. For at least a year and probably longer, we're still digging at it, Elinor Denovo was knifing him. She must have been a slick article. We can't find that she ever once actually mentioned his name, but last spring the only two clients he had that amounted to anything left him, and we have it in writing that they switched to a firm that was suggested and recommended by Elinor Denovo. Those are the two outstanding cases, but there are several others, and by the time it gets to trial we'll have a good file on it. As it stands now his lawyer would like to cop a plea for second-degree, but we want to wrap it up for first and I think we will. Evidently she decided, I think about a year and a half ago, to make it impossible for him to operate and she was doing a damn good job of it. You worked on him. Didn't you get any line on it?"

"No."

"You wouldn't withhold information."

"Sarcasm isn't your best blade, Mr. Cramer."

"That's why I never use it. And I doubt if you can use what I'm giving you. We've got a motive for Floyd Vance that's plenty good enough and it will be even better before we're through, but her motive for cooking him is your problem, not mine. It could be that she decided to even up for something that happened back in nineteen forty-four, but I'm glad we don't have to dig that deep. If you want to try, you're welcome, but Goodwin can't get him to come and spend another evening in that chair. He's not available."

"No. I was hoping for something useful, and apparently

I'll have to accept defeat. But I am obliged to you. Sincerely obliged."

"That's a line to hang up on," Cramer said, and hung up.

Wolfe took a deep breath and a corner of his mouth went up a full quarter of an inch. He looked at me and said, "Satisfactory."

"Satisfactory hell," I said, "it's perfect. Simply marvelous. Do I make out a check for Miss Denovo for twenty grand?"

"Not now. That may come later." He looked at the clock. "Get Mr. Jarrett. I'll talk."

My brows went up. "Father or son?"

"Mr. Cyrus M. Jarrett."

I nodded. "Yeah. I admit I'm fairly good at filling orders, but this time I need specifications. My batting record for getting Cyrus M. Jarrett to the phone is nothing for two. I *think* the person I get is named Oscar."

"I'll speak with Oscar."

My brows were up again as I swiveled, got the phone, and dialed area code 914 and a number. Wolfe had his receiver to his ear, so all my part needed was a finger, but I stayed on. After four rings the remembered male voice said, "Mr. Jarrett's residence."

"My name is Nero Wolfe. I am calling from New York. I wish to speak to Mr. Jarrett. Tell him—*don't interrupt me.* Tell him that I wish to speak with him about Floyd Vance. Repeat that name."

"But Mr. Jarrett is eating—"

"I told you to repeat that name. Floyd Vance."

"Floyd Vance."

"Good. Mr. Jarrett will be able to hear you. He doesn't eat with his ears. Tell him that I must speak with him *now* about Floyd Vance. You have my name?"

"Yes, sir."

"I'll hold the wire, but don't keep me waiting."

I probably wasn't breathing. It was a king-size gamble, and I was posting no odds. Too much depended on it. So the obvious step was drawing to what could be an inside straight. Not only was it possible that there was no close connection between Jarrett and Floyd Vance, and there was some other explanation for the checks Jarrett had

sent, it was even conceivable that he had never heard of
Floyd Vance. It could be that the next thing we would
hear would be Oscar, if it was Oscar, hanging up.

But it wasn't. I didn't time it because I was hanging on
a cliff, but I think it was about three hours. I mean three
minutes.

"You're interrupting my dinner."

I nodded at Wolfe. It was him.

"Mr. Jarrett?"

"Yes."

"My name is Nero Wolfe. I don't like to interrupt any
man's meal, but it's urgent. I have a decision to make
that can't be delayed. I just now conversed with the police
officer who is in charge of the investigation of the murder
of Elinor Denovo, and I can tell you in confidence that
Mr. Archie Goodwin, who has been to see you twice, and
I are responsible for the arrest of Floyd Vance as the
culprit. To justify a charge of first-degree murder the
police wish to establish a motive, and it is manifest that it
would help them to have your name so they can ask you
about the association of Floyd Vance and Elinor Denovo
twenty-three years ago. That would inevitably lead to your
appearance on the witness stand at the trial of Floyd
Vance, and I am reluctant to take the responsibility for
exposing a man of your standing to such an ordeal. Before
disclosing your name I would like to discuss the situation
with you, and I'll expect you here, at my office, at eleven
o'clock tomorrow morning."

"Was my name mentioned in your talk with the police
officer?"

"No."

"I know nothing about the association of Floyd Vance
and Elinor Denovo twenty-three years ago."

"Pfui. I'll call Mr. McCray at once and advise him to
make sure that certain checks in the files of the Seaboard
Bank and Trust Company are not disturbed. If the police
want them they can get a court order."

"Why should the police want them?"

"They customarily want everything that is, or may be,
relevant to a murder investigation. I can ask Inspector
Cramer's opinion after I have explained their significance.
Do you want me to do that?"

"No. If I had known the day Goodwin came . . ." He decided to let the if go. "I'll expect you here in the morning."

"I handle business only in my office. I am showing you more consideration than you deserve, sir. Will you be here tomorrow at eleven or not?"

"In the afternoon. Late afternoon."

"No. At eleven or not at all."

"At my age mornings are often difficult."

"Start it earlier. Rise earlier. At eleven or don't come."

"Damn you. I'll be there."

The connection went. I pushed the phone back, turned, and said, "I suppose you didn't lose an ounce. I lost ten pounds."

He grunted. "I'm not as phlegmatic as you think I am. It was that or nothing."

"Well, it's that. He's not only hooked, he's boated. Have you decided what the tie is? Him and Vance?"

"No."

"He's Vance's father."

He nodded. "That would be the most serviceable, for our purpose. Is there a noticeable resemblance?"

"Noticeable, no."

"That point isn't vital, but it would help to know. We will. On another point I need your opinion. Should Miss Denovo be here?"

"That *is* a point. She has been on my mind the last two days. I want to make a speech."

"Go ahead."

"She's a nice girl and a good client, and for a week I've been sorry we were going to have to tell her that Floyd Vance is her father. And since Tuesday morning I have been even sorrier. It's a damn shame that she has to know not only that such a character as Vance is her father but also that he killed her mother. I have thought of three possible ways to handle it without telling her, but none of them is really neat. I invite suggestions."

"I have none. I have an argument."

"Go ahead."

"I too have had reflections, if not identical with yours at least similar. It's desirable for a client to be satisfied not only with our performance but also with its result.

With Miss Denovo that's impossible. Circumstances forbid it. So the question is, What will dissatisfy her least? There are very few questions about any woman that I would undertake to answer with confidence, but you don't have that restraint and you know Miss Denovo. If she were offered the alternative, which would she choose? To know definitely that Floyd Vance, with all his grievous flaws, is her father? Or to remain all her life in the state of ignorance that brought her here three weeks ago with that money? Not how do you feel about her, but how would she feel?"

I didn't need to take a full minute to look at it, but I did, for the sake of appearances. "She would rather know," I said.

"Then she should be here tomorrow morning. In the alcove. Arrange it. Make certain that she will not intrude, no matter what she hears. You know her. Perhaps Saul should come to be with her. You will see him this evening?"

"I hope to. Depending on how long it takes to get her. She's loose now." I swung around to get the phone.

That was why I was late for poker. It was going on ten o'clock when I finally got Amy, at her apartment. Again I couldn't tell her anything, except to be at the office at half past ten in the morning, but at least that indicated that something was stirring. I told Saul ten-thirty too. The shape New York is in, you had better allow half an hour even with a Saul Panzer if you want to be sure.

16

I looked it up once. To eavesdrop means to stand under the eaves to listen to what is said inside a house. But to listen to what is said inside Wolfe's office you don't stand under the eaves; you stand in the alcove, which is at the rear end of the hall, to the left as you approach the kitchen. At eye level, if you are about the height of Wolfe or me, there is a rectangular hole in the wall, seven inches high and twelve inches wide. On the alcove side of the hole there is a panel which slides open silently, and on the office side there is a trick picture of a waterfall, "trick" because through the one-way picture you can not only eaves-hear from the alcove but also eaves-see nearly all of the office.

In arranging for Amy Denovo, who was eight inches shorter than me, to hear and see from the alcove I could have put phone books for her to stand on, but the show might last an hour or more, and for her price of admission of twenty grand she deserved something better than standing room. So after breakfast Friday morning I took the kitchen stepladder to the alcove, sat on it, and found that my eyes were five inches above the center of the hole. I had never measured Amy and me to determine how much of my extra eight inches was below the hips and how much was above, but I decided that would be close enough.

Amy arrived at 10:21 and Saul at 10:29. I took Amy to the alcove, had her perch on the stepladder, slid the panel open, and saw that her eyes were about right. "The size of that seat," I said, "it's a good thing it's your fanny and not Mr. Wolfe's."

142

"What *is* this?" she demanded.

"For you, spectator sport. You're going to hear and see he man who sent those two hundred and sixty-four hecks to your mother. Cyrus M. Jarrett is due at eleven 'clock, by appointment. We thought you ought to hear it irsthand, and with him in the red leather chair his face vill be about ten feet from yours. Take a look."

She leaned to get her eyes closer to the hole. "Won't he ee me?"

"No. From that side it's just a picture."

She turned to me. "But why do . . . What's he going o say?"

"We're waiting to hear him. Among other things he nay tell us, and you, the name of your father. That nay—"

The doorbell rang and I went, and it was Saul. I had old him what the program was and needed only to take him to the alcove and introduce him to the client who had paid him, through me, a little less than a grand in two weeks.

"Since you call me Archie," I told Amy, "you'll have to call him Saul not to hurt his feelings. He'll be here with you and if you get the idea that we're not asking Jarrett the right questions and decide to come and help, Saul will block you. Jarrett must not suspect that he has any audience but Mr. Wolfe and me. Have your shoes off, and if you feel a cough or a sneeze coming, for God's sake feel it soon enough to beat it to the kitchen." I looked at my watch. "He's due in twenty-five minutes, but he's driving ninety miles and he might be early. Saul will now take you to the kitchen for a coffee break. I'll be in the office taking tranquilizers to steady my nerves."

"You won't," Amy said.

"Then I won't," I said, and left them. It would take Saul about five minutes to get acquainted with her.

There had been one big danger. A man of Jarrett's position, financially and otherwise, might be able to put enough pressure on someone like the Police Commissioner or the Mayor or the New York Secretary of State, who issues private investigator licenses, to gag us. I blamed that fact, which had been on my mind ever since Jarrett had hung up, for something that had happened Thursday evening, when I had let Lon Cohen rake in a fat pot without showing, though it was at least three to two that my tens would have taken it. But now, as eleven o'clock came closer and closer, that danger got slimmer and slimmer, and it looked surer and surer that Jarrett's tie-in was so *very* personal that he couldn't risk it.

Wolfe came down at eleven on the dot, put the daily display in the vase on his desk, sat, and went at the morning mail. I had the expense book at my desk, checking entries and additions and getting totals, on the theory that they were final totals, except for Saul today. Just a pair of private detectives starting the daily grind, yeah. The reason they weren't holding their breath was that a man can't hold his breath more than about two minutes, and the doorbell didn't ring until a quarter past eleven.

The first two things I noticed when I opened the front door were that the car Jarrett had come in was a Heron town car, and that his eyes were exactly the same as they had been two weeks ago. I felt that I deserved a credit mark for the way I said, "Good morning." I could have made it a jab or even a jeer, but I swear it was just a cordial welcome.

He also said, "Good morning," but it wasn't a cordial anything. It was probably merely the way he had always said good morning, and always would, to everybody from the office boy to the senior vice-president. What was different from before was his walk as he went down the hall to the office. He didn't totter, but his steps were short and he made sure of each one before he took the next one. I waited until he had got safely lowered into the red leather chair to say, "Mr. Jarrett. Mr. Wolfe."

Jarrett said, "A footstool and a glass of water."

The only footstools in the house were in Fritz's room in the basement. On my way to the kitchen to ask to borrow it and tell him a glass of water was wanted, a glance showed me Saul and Amy in the alcove, and her shoes were off. In Fritz's big cluttered den in the basement, with its 294 cookbooks on eleven shelves, there were three footstools, and I took the biggest one, which was topped with a tapestry with a woven hunter aiming a spear at a woven wild boar.

Back up and in the office, I found that I hadn't missed

ny conversation. Jarrett was taking a large blue pill from
little gold box, and I stood with the footstool until he
ad put the pill in his mouth and got it down with a
wallow of water. He may have expected me to lift his
et to get the stool under, presumably Oscar would have,
ut I wasn't *that* cordial. After he got the glass back on
e stand he lifted them himself and I slid the stool under.

"There's a competent doctor a few doors away," Wolfe
aid.

"No," Jarrett said. The eyes were as frozen as ever
nd the bony jaw as set. "I told you mornings are difficult.
'alk."

Wolfe shook his head. "I will not hector a sick man.
Vill the pill help?"

"Damn your impudence." The bony jaw twitched. "I'm
ld. I'm not sick. You will not hector me, sick or well.
'alk."

Wolfe's shoulders went up a little and down. "Very
vell, sir, I'll talk, but it will go faster if you accept the
ealities of the situation. You say I won't hector you, but
already have. I bullied you into coming this morning,
nd in doing so I completely exposed my position. I made
t clear that you are faced with an alternative: either you
vill answer my questions about certain matters, answers
hat will satisfy me, or I will give the police information
hat will move them to investigate thoroughly your rela-
ions over the years with two people—Floyd Vance and
Carlotta Vaughn, later Elinor Denovo. If you are not
onversant with criminal law you may not know why the
police will be concerned. Floyd Vance's lawyer, if he
nows he can't get his client acquitted, and he can't, because of evidence supplied by Mr. Goodwin and me,
will try to get a verdict of accidental homicide or second-
degree murder. The police and the District Attorney will
want a verdict of first-degree murder, and to get it they
will need to establish a motive. You could verify this by
communicating with the police or the District Attorney,
but of course you can't do that, since you don't want the
details of your connection with those two people to be
disclosed. And they would inevitably be disclosed; once
the police get the concrete evidence of the connection, the
checks you sent to Elinor Denovo during those twenty-

three years, they will uncover all the facts. That's a task
for which they are admirably equipped."

Wolfe turned a hand over and said, with no change of
tone, "You had an early breakfast and a long ride. Will
you have refreshment of any kind? Coffee or other drink?
A sandwich, pastry, fruit? Thyme honey on corn fritters?"

Jarrett's jaw worked. "*Damn* your impudence." He ignored the offer of refreshments, which was a pity, for he
had never tasted Fritz's corn fritters coated with wild
thyme honey. "This is blackmail," he said, "but even if I
would pay, you couldn't deliver. If you don't tell the police
about those checks McCray will, or one of the others."

"No. Not possibly. They have no knowledge, not even
a suspicion, of any connection between you and Floyd
Vance. Only Mr. Goodwin and I have that."

"You do not. There is no connection. If you—"

"Mr. Jarrett. Don't talk nonsense. Accept the realities.
The mere mention of Floyd Vance's name brought you to
the telephone, and what I added brought you here. Pfui.
Confound it, you're not well."

It was something to see, how, in that fix, Jarrett's eyes
stayed as hard and cold as when he had told me I was an
idiot. "You're lying about McCray," he said. "He's behind
this and behind you."

"No. Only fools tell lies that are vulnerable. My sole
concern is the interest of my client, Miss Amy Denovo,
the daughter of Elinor Denovo."

"What do you want? How much?"

"I want nothing but answers to some questions. I want
the information that my client hired me to get, that's
all—and by the way, my commitment is a limited one. I
have engaged only to learn who and what her father was
—and is. I will be obliged to tell her only that, and no
other information you give me will be repeated to her or
to anyone else, either by Mr. Goodwin or by me."

Wolfe cocked his head. "You spoke of blackmail. Actually, as I said yesterday, I am showing you more consideration than you deserve. A citizen who possesses
information relevant to a crime is expected to give it to the
police. I could have done that yesterday and saved all
this pother. In their investigation they would certainly establish the identity of Amy Denovo's father and my

bligation to her would be met, and I would have earned
ly fee. I go to this unnecessary trouble only to gratify
ly self-esteem; I prefer to get the information myself,
irsthand. I don't want any thanks from you and don't
xpect any."

"You won't get any." Jarrett lifted his feet and kicked
he footstool aside. Evidently the pill had helped. "I an-
wer your questions and you earn your fee, and then you
nform the police."

"No. I have told you, except for the identity of Amy
Denovo's father, nothing that you say will be reported to
inyone, either by Mr. Goodwin or by me. If as assurance
of that you will not accept my word there was no point in
our coming."

Jarrett was visibly reacting. I admit it gave me pleasure
o see it, remembering the two sessions I had had with
iim. His jaw was working, the muscle at the side of his
ieck was twitching, and his fingers had folded to make
ists.

"Floyd Vance is Amy Denovo's father," he said.

Wolfe nodded. "As I surmised. How do you know that?"

"Damn you, I'm telling you! I know because . . . I have
personal knowledge. That's the information you say you
have been hired to get."

"It is indeed. But as I said, I must have answers that
satisfy me. We'll start at the beginning. In the spring of
nineteen forty-four Carlotta Vaughn left your employ and
went to work for and with Floyd Vance. Why?"

"I reserve details not essential for your satisfaction."

"Pfui. Sir, you are a man of sense. You say you are not
sick. Since you have declared your knowledge of the basic
fact, it's asinine to prolong this by trying to reserve details.
The decision on what will satisfy me is for me, not you.
This isn't an agreeable conversation for either of us, and
let's make it as brief as possible. Why did she leave you
and go to Floyd Vance?"

Jarrett's jaw had stopped working and the frozen eyes
were leveled at Wolfe. "I asked her to," he said. "I continued to pay her. She was very competent and I thought
she would put his business on a sound basis and straighten
him out. He didn't know she came from me. He knows
nothing about me. My communications to him and about

him have never been direct. My sending Carlotta Vaugh
to him was a mistake. When I returned from abroad i
September I learned what had happened. He had attracte
her and seduced her and she was pregnant. By then sh
had returned to her senses. She stayed on with him for
month or so, out of stubbornness, hoping to make a ma
of a fool, but it was impossible, even for her. She lef
She disappeared. I felt responsible, and I never slight
responsibility. I arranged to have her traced, but it too
months, and I learned of her change of name in Marc
nineteen forty-five. I arranged to keep informed, an
was, and I sent her a check shortly after the birth of he
child. I have not seen her or communicated with he
since October nineteen forty-four. I am giving you detai
that make it unnecessary for you to ask questions. I have n
knowledge of any contacts she may have had with Vanc
since October of nineteen forty-four. If he killed her
know nothing of his motive. I have never seen him or—
He stopped.

Wolfe asked, "Does he know he is your son?"

Jarrett was set for it and wasn't fazed. "I've answere
that," he said. "I said he knows nothing about me. Yo
don't merely assume that he is my son, you conclude i
because you can conceive of no other circumstance tha
would account for my taking the responsibility for Carlott
Vaughn's misfortune. To deny it would be pointless; yo
wouldn't believe me. If this Amy Denovo hires you t
learn more about her father I know what you'll do, an
I've had enough of you. His mother's name was Florenc
Vance. In nineteen fourteen she was twenty and I wa
twenty-three. She was a waitress in a restaurant in Boston
She died five days after the child was born. No; Floyd
Vance does not know I am his father. If you have
material question ask it."

"There are many I could ask," Wolfe said, "but yo
have covered the essential points. It is only my curiosit
that would be satisfied by knowing how you got word t
Floyd Vance, two weeks ago, that I was looking for Am
Denovo's father, and I can't insist on that. I do have
comment. If you had told Mr. Goodwin when he firs
called on you what you have just told me, it is extremel
likely that Floyd Vance would never have been identified

as the murderer of Elinor Denovo. Also Amy Denovo's problem would have been solved and she would not have to pay me for two weeks of strenuous effort. You say you never slight a responsibility. You are clearly responsible for the added strain and expense my client has had to bear. If you send me a check in payment for the work I have done for her, I will return the retainer she gave me and charge her nothing. Should you decide to do that, the amount is fifty thousand dollars. If you do, or if you don't, it will add to my knowledge of my fellow man. Archie, that chair is hard to rise from. Mr. Jarrett may want your arm."

He didn't. I went, but he ignored me. He pulled his feet in, swung his torso forward in a kind of lunge, and made it. The blue pill must have had something. I'll say this for him, he never wasted words. No other man I had ever met would have simply let Wolfe's comments ride, but he did. That was the third time I saw him make an abrupt exit, and the big difference was that the first two times the exit line had been his. Walking out, his step was surer than it had been coming in. I got to the hall ahead of him, and to the front door. When he appeared on the stoop the chauffeur opened the door of the Heron and crossed the sidewalk and started up, but Jarrett shook his head and made it down alone, and the chauffeur didn't offer to help him in. Evidently he knew the signs.

As the Heron rolled I shut the door, went to the alcove, and said, "I hope you could hear all right. We can't report or repeat anything."

Saul slid the panel shut. Amy, leaving the stool, misjudged the distance to the floor and landed off balance. I took her arm, and she said, "Thank you," politely. Her cheeks had less color than usual.

I said politely, "You're welcome. You heard all right?"

"Yes. I don't . . . Do you mind if I go now?"

"Certainly not. How about an escort? Saul or me."

"I'd rather not. I don't want to talk. I don't . . . feel like it. When I get . . . I'll give you a ring. But I have already decided one thing. My mother named me Amy Denovo, and that's my name."

"Good for you."

"I don't have to see him now, do I? I don't want to."

"Of course not. He's probably settled back, reading a book about Germany. Ring me any time."

She turned and started off but was blocked by Saul coming from the kitchen. "Your shoes," he said.

"Thank you," she said politely, and took my arm with her left hand while she put them on with her right. "Don't come," she said, and went.

When the door had closed behind her Saul said, "She took it fine. Don't pay me for today. I wasn't needed."

17

The purpose of this footnote is to add to your knowledge of your fellow man. Cyrus M. Jarrett's check for fifty grand—personal, not a bank check—came in the mail on January twenty-sixth, three days after the jury brought in their first-degree verdict on Floyd Vance.

ABOUT THE AUTHOR

REX STOUT, the creator of Nero Wolfe, was born in Noblesville, Indiana, in 1886, the sixth of nine children of John and Lucetta Todhunter Stout, both Quakers. Shortly after his birth, the family moved to Wakarusa, Kansas. He was educated in a country school, but, by the age of nine, was recognized throughout the state as a prodigy in arithmetic. Mr. Stout briefly attended the University of Kansas, but left to enlist in the Navy, and spent the next two years as a warrant officer on board President Theodore Roosevelt's yacht. When he left the Navy in 1908, Rex Stout began to write freelance articles, worked as a sightseeing guide and as an itinerant bookkeeper. Later he devised and implemented a school banking system which was installed in four hundred cities and towns throughout the country. In 1927 Mr. Stout retired from the world of finance and, with the proceeds of his banking scheme, left for Paris to write serious fiction. He wrote three novels that received favorable reviews before turning to detective fiction. His first Nero Wolfe novel, *Fer-de-Lance*, appeared in 1934. It was followed by many others, among them, *Too Many Cooks, The Silent Speaker, If Death Ever Slept, The Doorbell Rang* and *Please Pass the Guilt*, which established Nero Wolfe as a leading character on a par with Erle Stanley Gardner's famous protagonist, Perry Mason. During World War II, Rex Stout waged a personal campaign against Nazism as chairman of the War Writers' Board, master of ceremonies of the radio program "Speaking of Liberty" and as a member of several national committees. After the war, he turned his attention to mobilizing public opinion against the wartime use of thermonuclear devices, was an active leader in the Authors' Guild and resumed writing his Nero Wolfe novels. All together, his Nero Wolfe novels have been translated into twenty-two languages and have sold more than forty-five million copies. Rex Stout died in 1975 at the age of eighty-eight. A month before his death, he published his forty-sixth Nero Wolfe novel, *A Family Affair*.

NERO WOLFE

He's not much to look at and he'll never win the hundred yard dash but for sheer genius at unraveling the tangled skeins of crime he has no peer. His outlandish adventures make for some of the best mystery reading in paperback. He's the hero of these superb suspense stories.

BY REX STOUT

THE THRILLING AND MASTERFUL NOVELS OF ROSS MACDONALD

Winner of the Mystery Writers of America Grand Master Award, Ross Macdonald is acknowledged around the world as one of the greatest mystery writers of our time. *The New York Times* has called his books featuring private investigator Lew Archer "the finest series of detective novels ever written by an American."

Now, Bantam Books is reissuing Macdonald's finest work in handsome new paperback editions. Look for these books (a new title will be published every month) wherever paperbacks are sold or use the handy coupon below for ordering:

Masters *of* Mystery

With these new mystery titles, Bantam takes you to the scene of the crime. These masters of mystery follow in the tradition of the Great British and American crime writers. You'll meet all these talented sleuths as they get to the bottom of even the most baffling crimes.

☐	24605	NOTHING CAN RESCUE ME Elizabeth Daly	$2.50
☐	24610	THE HOUSE WITHOUT THE DOOR Elizabeth Daly	$2.50
☐	24616	AND DANGEROUS TO KNOW Elizabeth Daly	$2.50
☐	24190	FLOWERS FOR THE JUDGE Margery Allingham	$2.95
☐	23780	HARRIET FAREWELL Margaret Erskine	$2.50
☐	24852	DANCERS IN MOURNING Margery Allingham	$2.95
☐	23783	CASE WITH THREE HUSBANDS Margaret Erskine	$2.50
☐	23605	TETHER'S END Margery Allingham	$2.50
☐	23590	BLACK PLUMES Margery Allingham	$2.50
☐	23822	TRAITOR'S PURSE Margery Allingham	$2.50
☐	23496	THE WRONG WAY DOWN Elizabeth Daly	$2.50
☐	23669	EVIDENCE OF THINGS SEEN Elizabeth Daly	$2.50
☐	23811	THE BOOK OF THE CRIME Elizabeth Daly	$2.50

SPECIAL
MONEY SAVING
OFFER

Now you can have an up-to-date listing of Bantam's hundreds of titles plus take advantage of our unique and exciting bonus book offer. A special offer which gives you the opportunity to purchase a Bantam book for only 50¢. Here's how!

By ordering any five books at the regular price per order, you can also choose any other single book listed (up to a $4.95 value) for just 50¢. Some restrictions do apply, but for further details why not send for Bantam's listing of titles today!

Just send us your name and address plus 50¢ to defray the postage and handling costs.